A Healing Rain

Crawdad Beach Series, Book 12

Lisa Buffaloe

Crawdad Beach novels may be enjoyed as a series
or read as a standalone.

A Healing Rain

Visit the author's website at https://lisabuffaloe.com.

Cover Design: JoAnn Durgin

ISBN: 978-1-957715-52-0 (eBook)
ISBN: 978-1-957715-53-7 (Paperback)
ISBN: 978-1-957715-54-4 (Hardcover)

A Healing Rain

Rain Day has been on a restless journey, moving from place to place, away from her embarrassing past, searching for something she can't quite define.

A near-death experience sparks a need for a stable life, bringing her to the small community of Crawdad Beach. Rain hopes to find peace and a place to call home, but her journey is far from over.

Vic Caine's facial scar is a visible reminder of his earlier mistakes. Seeking a quieter life away from his troubled past, he makes the move to Crawdad Beach.

Unexpected danger brings Rain and Vic together. As they navigate internal and external challenges, will they trust God, find healing from their past and discover the strength and courage needed for the future?

Join Rain and Vic in this heartwarming tale of faith, love, and second chances.

"A Healing Rain" is a story that will inspire you to believe in the power of healing and the beauty of new beginnings.

Table of Contents

Chapter 1

Rain Day stood on the bank of the mountain river that ran clear and cold from the early spring snowmelt.

Water flowed over and around the boulders, smoothed by the relentless current, reminding her of her own restless journey. Since college, she'd been a whirlwind of movement, traipsing from one place to another.

Yet, no matter where she went, something remained missing, like searching for a wisp of smoke in the wind.

Rain scanned the area. Where was her dog, Lightning? She let out a loud whistle.

A flash of white fur rocketed from the forest's edge. A happy yelp announced her dog's arrival. He screeched to a stop by her side, tail thumping a joyful rhythm against the ground.

Rain patted his furry head. "Hey, boy. Where have you been?"

Lightning let out a muffled bark as though answering her question.

She chuckled as she rubbed his fur. Her dog was a thirty-five-pound mutt that thought he was the embodiment of a warrior. He didn't walk; he strutted. He didn't run; he zoomed. And to top off his fun qualities, Lightning was an excellent judge of character who protected her no matter what came her way.

With her dog by her side, Rain walked alongside the river as the afternoon sunshine cast playful shadows on the ground. She inhaled the earthy fragrance of pine and damp soil filling the air.

Her phone buzzed with an incoming message. So much for a peaceful walk without interruptions. Rain stopped and took her phone out of her backpack to check.

Her parents had sent the latest photos from their life in Zurich, Switzerland. They never discussed their work, only that they were grateful to be involved in cutting-edge technology.

Rain scrolled through the pictures, admiring the majestic mountains and the vibrant colors of the scenery they sent. It was funny how her parents kept in touch more since moving two years ago across the ocean than they did when she and her brother were kids.

Her parents, two scientists employed by a medical firm, had attempted to balance work and family but fell short in their parenting duties. Not because they were mean or abusive; they were just . . . clueless.

Quirky.

Cerebral.

Pretty much forgetful about anything outside of work.

Her parents hadn't even planned what they would name their children before they were born. Birthed on an overcast day, her brother, two years older, received the name Sonny Les Day. As for her, she'd come into the world on a rainy day and thus been named Rain E Day. She didn't have a middle name, except for a simple 'E'.

Rain bit back a chuckle at the thought. With names like that, she and Sonny had to grow up tough and with a sense of humor. Despite their parents' eccentricities, they knew they were loved.

She turned to the river as a backdrop and sent a smiling photo of herself, along with a note about where she was staying, before moving on.

Lightning let out a sharp bark; his ears perked up at something above them.

Rain scanned the sky. A flash of black zoomed quickly out of view. She patted Lightning. "Whatever it was, it looks like you scared it off."

With a victorious puff, the dog strutted around her, as though he owned the world.

Tucking her phone into her backpack, Rain continued her riverside stroll. Further downstream, a forty-five-foot waterfall cascaded from a rocky cliff. She couldn't resist revisiting it today. The sheer power of the water was incredible to watch as it crashed against the rocks below, creating a breathtaking display of nature's might.

The thunderous roar of the falls filled her ears as she

approached the point where the water fell over the cliffs. Rain placed her backpack beside a nearby tree with instructions for Lightning to stay.

She moved closer to the river's edge. The waterfall spray was an exhilarating dance, each drop a tiny kiss of pure bliss. Infused with the water's power, she raised her hands and took another tiny step closer.

The ground crumbled beneath her feet.

With a scream, Rain tumbled into the cold, rushing water.

The sound of the falls deafened as she thrashed, desperately trying to reach something to save herself.

The swift and unforgiving current pulled her under, the world spinning and tumbling.

Rain's head broke the surface of the water. She gasped, her lungs burning for air.

Clawing at the slippery rocks, the current tugged and pulled with relentless force. Her body slammed against the rough surface of a boulder, the impact knocking the breath from her lungs.

She was going to die.

A hand, calloused and strong, seized Rain's arm, pulling her through the thrashing water until she collapsed onto the shore.

Water streamed from her long hair as she coughed and expelled what had been trapped in her lungs. Struggling to breathe, she could hear a deep voice whispering that she was now safe.

Two powerful arms encircled her, their grip firm yet gentle, lifting her smoothly from the ground.

Rain forced her eyes open. A man. His handsome features blurry except for his intense blue eyes and a jagged scar that slashed across his cheek.

She tried to stay awake and alert, but her vision blurred and faded to gray. Then black.

With a groan, she pried her eyes open, and her surroundings came into view. How did she get here? A blanket around her shoulders, she sat in the worn wooden rocker on the porch of her rented cabin. Her backpack and trusty dog sat beside her.

As she looked toward Lightning, his tail thumped a happy rhythm against the wooden porch.

How did her rescuer know where she was staying?

Even stranger, she didn't feel uneasy about his knowing. If her dog hadn't attacked him, the man must have been okay.

Rain groaned as she got to her feet. She unlocked the door of her cabin, stumbled inside, and collapsed on the bed as Lightning snuggled next to her.

Who was her rescuer, and why had her life been spared?

Maybe God hadn't given up on her yet.

Vic Caine, still buzzing with adrenaline, retrieved his drone and controls from the forest floor and headed back to his Jeep. If he hadn't been taking a video and photos of the waterfall, he wouldn't have been there to save the woman.

Vic opened his tailgate and placed the drone in the back. With a gentle click, he unhooked the camera and carefully placed it in his padded equipment box.

What if he hadn't gotten there in time? What if she had gone over the falls? Vic ran a hand through his close-cut hair.

His parents didn't believe in chance or luck; they would tell him that God had put him there to save that girl. He would agree with them. There were too many coincidences.

The roar of the water had been deafening as he launched himself across the slick boulders, grabbing her arm just as she was about to be swept over the falls.

Adrenaline fading, Vic leaned against his open tailgate, the cool metal a welcome contrast to his still-racing pulse.

He'd spent the last two days filming and photographing the area for a survey of the property. Being in the quiet, away from the crowds, helped him center.

Vic had noticed the woman and her dog when she left the cabin, and how she seemed drawn to the forest, river, and the falls. Was she renting the place, or was she related to the owner? Whatever her story, he was grateful he had been there to help.

Vic got in his Jeep and drove to the hotel where he was staying. He needed to get the videos and photos edited to deliver to his client. Once he met his customer, Vic could collect his payment and then head to see his friend in Crawdad Beach.

He was tired of living in his hometown of Charlotte. The city had grown too large and congested and held too many unpleasant memories. With his online website, he could find plenty of work for his drone photography and surveying, no matter where he lived.

Vic's thoughts returned to the beautiful woman he'd rescued. Maybe he should have stayed until she woke up, but with her dog there, he knew she'd be safe.

Plus, what would she want with a scar-faced man?

Chapter 2

Crisp morning air filled Rain's lungs as she strolled along the trail leading back to the cabin. The shadow of the trees, the darkness of the forest, partially dampened light and sound.

In the woods, the world slowed, and she could breathe.

Rain stopped, her eyes drawn to the raw, splintered wood where a branch had torn from a tree, leaving a ragged scar.

Like the man who saved her.

Who was he? Why hadn't he stayed around to introduce himself? Maybe he was just an illusion.

Rain shook her head. No, someone had rescued her. There was no way she could have been saved from going over the falls without help.

Perhaps she had a handsome, scar-faced guardian angel.

As much trouble as she got into as a kid, that would probably fit. Her mom said even as a baby, Rain stayed in motion. She didn't know why she'd always been restless, wanting something different, to see something new.

Rain walked on. The tree-lined trail opened, and the charming cabin she'd rented came into view, with a meadow of colorful wildflowers blooming behind. With a sigh, she settled into the worn rocker on the front porch.

If only she could stay here and live full-time in nature's beauty. Unfortunately, the cabin's owner was returning, and she had to get moving again.

The prospect of venturing into the unknown once held a powerful allure.

Now?

Not so much.

Her tiny RV, complete with a comfortable sleeping area, small bathroom, and the technology she needed for her job, gave her the freedom to travel and work from anywhere. As a graphic computer artist, digital creator, and a dabbler in AI technology, she had plenty of clients.

Rain leaned her head back on the rocker. Maybe her near-death experience caused the lack of travel enthusiasm, or perhaps she was just getting older. She was twenty-three, and her parents had raised her to be virtually self-sufficient by the time she was nine years old.

With a sharp bark, Lightning zoomed to where a squirrel perched on a high limb chattering, its bushy tail twitching. The dog responded with growls and barks while circling the base of the tree.

Rain stood and stretched her back. It was time to find a place of her own, a cabin in the woods where she and

Lightning could enjoy nature without having to travel.

When her grandparents passed away, they left her and Sonny a generous inheritance, enough to provide a comfortable life for both of them. Her brother, now newly married, used his share to buy his first home in Charleston, South Carolina.

Rain went inside to pack her bags. Her online friends had given her plenty of ideas of where to settle, from beach to mountain locations. She enjoyed viewing the ocean, but she got seasick and disliked storms, as well as the pervasive sand that worked its way into shoes, clothes, and any opening in skin.

She placed Lightning's food and water bowls, along with his favorite blanket, into his travel bag. The mountains were great, but the isolation could be a bit much. In contrast, civilization meant easy access to supermarkets and a limitless supply of hot coffee.

Another location idea came from a woman who'd helped handle a hacker who had attacked Rain's website. Stella, the website fixer, mentioned that Crawdad Beach was a great place to live. The town wasn't on the ocean, but was within driving distance.

Rain shoved a stray hair behind her ear. Why would she want to live in a small town?

Switzerland was out of the question. Too far for both her and her dog. Especially since her parents kept in better touch via texting than in person.

She didn't want to live close to her married brother. Rain loved Sonny's wife, but they needed time alone as they navigated the newlywed life. Plus, their constant lovey-dovey stuff was rather nauseating and made her envious.

Rain folded her clothes, smoothing out each wrinkle before placing them into her travel bag. She'd dated on and off throughout high school and college. Even had a boyfriend with the last name of Knight, but she couldn't see herself going from Day to Knight.

She'd even been engaged for a few weeks until she discovered it was all a gag, and she was the brunt of the joke.

Men.

She didn't need them. Her dog was her ever-faithful companion.

With everything packed, Rain cast one last glance around the cabin. She'd only been here a week, but she could have stayed forever.

Setting her belongings on the porch, Rain locked the door behind her. Lightning, still sitting under the tree, glanced a curious look her way.

"Yep, it's time to get moving."

With a joyous bark, Lightning zoomed to her, his paws padding softly on the ground as he danced around her feet.

At least her dog was excited about their trip.

She just wished she knew where to go.

Vic made another pass along the brick-paved main street of Crawdad Beach. For a small town, it certainly had a lot of visitors. He had to circle twice before he could find a place to park. People of all ages ambled along the sidewalks as though no one was in a hurry.

He found a space in front of Doohickeys Hardware. Their sign stated they offered a wide range of building supplies, hardware, and whatever whatchamacallit needed. What do you know? He'd finally located a store that could help him despite his inability to name hardware items.

Vic checked the time. He still had twenty minutes to spare before meeting with his online buddy, Marcus Paterson, at Rolling in the Dough Bakery.

Crawdad Beach had a surprising variety of businesses in its two-story brick buildings. Besides the bakery, the town featured a post office, Knick Knacks Antique store, Curl and Dye Beauty Salon, Tiddlywinks Restaurant, loft apartments, Hotel de Crawdad, a medical clinic, and a law office.

On his drive through the area, he'd noticed a decent-sized supermarket and a church. There were even several new homes under construction.

Not bad.

It looked as though Crawdad Beach offered everything he might need.

Vic stopped outside an old building that had been transformed into loft apartments. Noting the website location for inquiries, he took his phone, entered the information, and read the listing. From the photos, the apartments looked great and were surprisingly affordable.

Interesting. He'd be close enough to several large cities, the ocean, a state park, and still be within driving distance for family functions.

Besides being a licensed surveyor, his drone work and photography gave him a decent income., and he had the freedom to live wherever he chose.

The endless work, road trips, and impersonal motel rooms had left him drained and longing for something more stable.

Could he earn a good living without constant travel and be content in a small town?

Vic put his phone in his back pocket as he turned toward the bakery to meet up with his friend. He glanced around. An older man and woman walked hand in hand. A group of older women chatted about husbands and their families as they walked past. A young couple with a small girl entered the restaurant.

How would a single guy like him fit into a family-oriented place like this? Maybe small-town life wasn't for him after all.

Vic rubbed the scar on the side of his face. Women either pitied him or, finding out about his military service, concluded that combat duty had scarred his face. Unfortunately, he couldn't claim that as accurate.

Every morning as he shaved, the scar served as an ever-present reminder of his reckless and stupid behavior.

Chapter 3

"What do you think?" Rain pointed to her computer screen showing the listing of a cabin she'd found online.

Lightning lifted his head off the RV floor, his eyes half-open, then with a grunt settled back down to rest.

"Fine, I'll keep looking." Rain continued scrolling through the real estate site. Surely she could find an affordable cabin with a plot of land where they could live.

Places like that were all over the country, but she wanted to be close enough to visit Sonny and his wife, Holly. Evidently, log cabins weren't as popular in South Carolina as they were in other regions.

Rain sighed. She needed to adjust her wish list. Maybe she could find a cute little house with a covered porch. And since she was considering living in the South, a screened-in back patio would be a nice addition.

She filled out her requirements on the real estate site. Eighty-three properties popped up on the screen, but most weren't even close to what she was hoping to find.

Then she saw it.

A listing for a small gray barndominium with white trim, three years old, that sat on a wooded acre. Even better, the property was within walking distance of a state park with a lake.

Why was she so drawn to the place? She always thought she'd have a log cabin somewhere in the mountains. Yet still, a surge of anticipation coursed through her as she scanned the photos. A covered porch wrapped around the front and right side. A carport located in the rear, connected to another covered patio area. Hmmm. She could hire someone to screen in part of that section.

She clicked on the next photos. The house inside had high ceilings, rustic barn doors, two bedrooms, two bathrooms, a family room with a fireplace, a nice kitchen and dining area, and a laundry room with a sink for washing her dog. Laminated wood-look flooring throughout the house would be perfect with Lightning.

The baby barndominium was even within her price range. Maybe, just maybe, she'd found a place to call her own.

"Lightning, what about this one?"

Her dog's ears perked as he lifted his head and seemed to study the screen. His tail gave a happy wag.

"Okay, let's see what we need to find out."

Rain checked the property's location. Well, what do you know? It was only a few miles from Crawdad Beach, the town her online friend had mentioned. Plus, the location would still be close enough to visit her brother.

If she bought the place, her fur baby could play and roam, and she could set up her office in the second bedroom.

Rain nibbled on a fingernail. Just because the house looked nice online, was she ready to buy something and settle?

Before she did anything, she needed to see the property in person and check out Crawdad Beach.

Rain closed the open tabs on her computer and moved to the front of the RV. Tail-wagging, Lightning jumped into the passenger seat.

The idea of finally having her own place filled her with a long-forgotten excitement. She even had happy goosebumps popping up on her arms.

Plugging the destination into her GPS, Rain started up her vehicle and pulled onto the road.

For her first thirteen years, she grew up in a typical American town, on a typical street in a typical brick two-story home with a two-car garage, two parents, two kids, two cars, and two goldfish, who, oddly enough, seemed to change colors and even size and shape every few months.

Rain discovered later that when a fish passed on to the great fishbowl in the sky, her parents wouldn't say anything; they'd just replace it with a new one.

If she bought the baby barndominium, she could decorate and landscape the way she wanted, and no fish would die on her watch.

Mouth-watering smells of fresh bakery products and sugary glaze surrounded Vic as he stepped into Rolling in the Dough Bakery.

He grinned at the wall decoration of a cartoon crawdad wearing a teal apron and holding a rolling pin with one claw and an oven mitt in the other. A display case of old bakery tools and a teal bicycle were on the other walls. His mom would love the place.

Vic's eyes darted around the tables, seeking his friend, who from the photo he'd sent wore glasses and had dark hair and eyes. He spotted Marcus sitting by the front window, engrossed in his laptop screen.

Stepping up to the glass-front display cases, Vic surveyed the variety of donuts, cupcakes, muffins, cookies, cakes, and something called a Crawdad Claw.

Behind the counter, a cute brown-haired woman close to his age smiled. "May I help you?"

"Yeah, what's a Crawdad Claw?"

She grinned. "It's our version of what most people know as a bear claw."

"Looks good to me. I'll take one and a cup of black coffee."

"Coming right up." She turned to fill his order.

"Vic!" Marcus came up behind him and slapped him on the back. "Nice to meet you in person."

"Same here." Vic shook his friend's outstretched hand.

"The food's great, and the sexy owner is amazing." Marcus wiggled his eyebrows at the woman behind the counter.

"Thanks for the comment, you big hunk of a man," the woman came from behind the counter, wrapped her arms around Marcus, and kissed him with gusto.

Vic rubbed the back of his neck and stepped back. What was happening?

Marcus grinned at Vic. "This is my wife, Olivia."

Vic let out a nervous chuckle. "I was wondering."

Olivia smiled. "Nice to meet you, Vic. Welcome to Crawdad Beach."

"The town is friendly," Marcus added with a chuckle. "But I don't recommend kissing someone you don't know."

"I'll keep that in mind," Vic said. He'd never be confident enough to kiss a woman like that.

Olivia handed Vic his pastry and coffee. "No charge. We're glad you're here."

"Thanks," Vic followed Marcus to his table.

While Vic munched on his crawdad claw, Marcus enthusiastically described all the good things about the town, painting a picture of the happy and fulfilled life Vic could have.

Vic shook his head. "You sound like you're on the

Crawdad Beach publicity team."

"Sorry about that." Marcus grinned. "I enjoy being here. I think you would too. The loft apartments are great if you're interested. You know, I met Olivia here in town." Marcus turned an appreciative gaze in his wife's direction.

Vic took a sip of his coffee. He doubted he'd find anyone who would want to be his wife. For him, dating had been a series of disappointments.

His ever-positive parents had named him Victor to remind him that all things are possible for God and that he could be victorious with God's help.

He went instead by Vic, a name he'd chosen intentionally after the incident in high school. Sure, he'd been successful with his school grades, the military, and work, but his romantic life was a different story.

Still, Crawdad Beach did seem like a decent place to settle. He could move here, stay in the apartments for a few months, then find a house on a plot of land.

If God did care for him, maybe he'd even find a woman with terrible eyesight unbothered by his scar.

Vic gulped down his coffee. Probably best to buy a dog. A male dog, unconcerned with his appearance, who would be loyal to the end.

Chapter 4

Did she really want to do this? Move and stay somewhere?

Rain drove along a country road, pine trees creating a green tunnel on either side. Blacktop or gravel driveways appeared every few miles, winding their way towards houses and farms of varying sizes.

The road crossed under an interstate leading to a popular beach town. At the intersection stood a bank, a pharmacy, a fast-food place, a hotel, and a sprawling all-in-one store. To the right, a sign pointed towards an industrial park.

Rain continued driving. A small bridge crossed over an inlet waterway that seemed like only a small sandy river. A sign directed to Wilderness State Park, touting its 200-acre lake with camping, cabin rentals, and walking trails.

Nice. That park must be the one near the house she'd seen online. A slow-moving tractor ahead, Rain tapped her brakes to match its leisurely pace. The old man in the driver's seat raised his weathered hand and signaled for her to pass.

With a friendly beep of her horn, she waved as she

drove around him.

At first, the joy of traveling around the country had been intoxicating, but the thrill had faded. She was restless of being restless.

Sure, she had a place to sleep and work, but living in a small RV wasn't for the faint of heart.

Rain rolled down the front windows, feeling the warm wind whip through her hair as she continued along the country road. Pure delight was visible on Lightning's face as he stuck his head out the passenger window.

Her new goals included having her own bedroom, bathroom with a soaker tub, kitchen, a washer and dryer, and a comfortable space to unwind, work, and feel at home.

Rain slowed as she neared her destination. Small farms and widely spaced houses dotted the country road. She stopped across the street from the baby barndominium.

While the building appeared spacious from the outside, the square footage listing said otherwise. Still, maybe she should have looked for something smaller before working her way up to 1650 square feet.

"What do you think?" Rain asked Lightning.

Her dog's ears perked; he stared past her out the side window.

"If I bought this place, would you be happy here? We wouldn't have to travel as much."

As Lightning looked back and forth between her and the house, his tail wagged, and he gave her a cheerful bark.

"Okay. I'll call the realtor." Rain reviewed the listing, found the agent's contact information, and then tapped in the number on her phone.

After the call ended, she grinned at Lightning. "Looks like we have about fifteen minutes to explore before the realtor can get here."

Rain pulled back onto the road. As it curved, the sparkling expanse of a lake came into view. With the property this close to the water, they could come down here anytime they liked.

A flat spot near the road was the ideal place to pull over and take Lightning for a quick walk.

She parked and then snapped on his leash. "Let's go explore."

Lightning walked differently when he was happy. His paws seemed to skip with joy as they strolled near the sandy shoreline of the lake.

A tiny sailboat with a vibrant sail drifted lazily on the water. Farther across the lake, the spray from two jet-skis created a shimmering mist.

The area seemed perfect. Her parents would tell her she should pray before making a big decision.

Rain glanced up at the fluffy white clouds drifting across the sky's blue canvas. She hated to admit, even to herself, that she hadn't talked much to God lately. Not that she was mad at Him or anything like that, she just wasn't sure He wanted to hear from her.

From time to time, Rain would slip into a church to check in with God, ask again for His forgiveness. She'd even watch online sermons by her favorite preacher.

She'd wandered from God, but never wanted to be too far away.

Enjoying the warm sunshine on her shoulders, Rain led Lightning along a path that led by the lake. God was probably still upset at her for her college exploits during her freshman year and the relationships she had with people she should have avoided. Her insecurities had made a mess of things, putting her in situations that still made her cringe.

Dating the good-looking, smooth-talking, university photographer had been her biggest problem. Rain had been with him on the sidelines during her college football's last big rivalry game.

During the remaining few minutes of the game, while walking on the sidelines, she'd stumbled. Not only did she trip; she slipped, stumbled, and tumbled until she landed in a heap beside the one-yard line, just as a player lunged to catch the ball for the winning score.

Her presence distracted the player, causing him to fumble, which led to their team losing the big rivalry game, broadcast for all the world to see.

Rain became the most hated person in her school's

history. The news headlines in the papers and all over social media announced that the university lost the big game due to falling rain.

She grimaced at the unpleasant memories.

Her dog stared intently at a fish bobbing near the shimmering water. Lightning pounced.

With a flick of its tail, the tiny fish darted away.

Rain sighed. Just like time had slipped away from her. If she could return to the past, she'd do many things differently. Of course, knowing her luck, she'd attempt to fix her past mistakes, wind up tripping, and create an even bigger mess.

Back at her RV, she dried her soaking dog with a towel.

God had spared her from going over the falls. Had He given her a second chance?

After buckling her seatbelt, Rain returned to the barndominium. If only God would give her a sign so she could stop running.

Fushia Gates, the realtor, met Rain on the front porch. The woman removed the key from the lockbox hanging on the doorknob. "I know you'll love this charming custom-built home just minutes away from Crawdad Beach and the State Park."

Mrs. Gates's multiple bracelets jangled as she opened the door and dramatically swept her hand. "The house includes open-concept living with soaring ceilings and granite countertops in the kitchen."

Rain took a deep breath as she walked around the family room. Even though it was three years old, it still smelled new, and the house seemed serene, as if those who lived there had been at peace.

A stone fireplace dominated the family room, set between expansive windows that framed the vibrant green grass and towering trees behind the house.

Mrs. Gates moved in unison with her, their footsteps echoing in the quiet. "The house has two bedrooms, two baths, and an upstairs room you could use as an office, bedroom, or playroom. The covered porches are for you to enjoy the beauty of the property. At 1650 square feet, this home is a rare mix of style, space, and serenity."

"It's really nice," Rain said as she walked through the kitchen. "Do the appliances stay?"

"Yes, everything but the furniture would be yours." Mrs. Gates lowered her voice as though someone might overhear what she was saying. "My clients have already moved to a new job in Charlotte. The furniture here is just for staging the house. They are the sweetest young couple, and even though they loved their home, they are eager to sell and start their new life."

Appreciative of the extra information, Rain stepped out onto the covered back patio and was delighted to see fans installed in the ceiling. Making it into a screened-in porch would be perfect.

Rain paused to admire the trees, their leaves casting cool shadows that framed the green lawn. She went back inside to the main bedroom.

Above the bed, elegant calligraphy displayed the words, *Peace I leave you, My peace I give you; not as the world gives, do I give to you. Do not let your hearts be troubled, nor fearful ~ John 14:27.*

Was that her sign? Was God telling her this was the place to start over?

She walked to the second bedroom, furnished as an office.

Goosebumps raised on her arms as she stared at the calligraphy inscribed on the wall above the desk, *Come to me, all you who are weary and burdened, and I will give you rest ~ Matthew 11:28.*

Rain turned to the realtor. "Mrs. Gates, I'll take it."

Chapter 5

Vic took one last look around his apartment in Charlotte. With his belongings loaded into the rental truck and his Jeep hitched to the rear, he was ready to go.

Even though Vic's brother thought he was crazy to move to a smaller town, both of them had spent the morning loading up the truck. Vic locked the apartment and made his way to the office to turn in his key.

He hoped he wasn't making a mistake with this move. He did want a quieter lifestyle, and Crawdad Beach seemed like the place for a welcome change. Anyway, it wasn't like he had a line of women hoping to go out with him.

Vic paused at the apartment's swimming pool, its blue water shimmering in the sunlight. He was not a fan of the nightlife scene; instead, he'd enjoyed taking laps in the evenings. Maybe he'd find something else to do after work.

He made his way to the office. As he stepped inside, the attractive blonde he'd seen on his previous visits sat behind her desk. Her smile was flirtatious as her eyes met his. "Hi, Vic."

"Hi." Surprised she knew his name, he stood there like an idiot, racking his brain, but her name was nowhere to be found. "I'm turning in my key." Vic laid it on her desk and stepped back.

"You're leaving?" She rose to her feet and moved close to where he stood. "I'm sorry we didn't get to know one another better." The faint scent of her perfume wrapped around him.

"Yeah, sorry about that," Vic muttered as heat ignited the back of his neck. "I've got to go." He hurried out of the door and mentally slapped himself on the head.

What an idiot. Why didn't he stay and talk to her?

What was the use?

He was leaving, and she was probably flirting with him because he wouldn't be around.

A woman like her would never want to be with someone like him.

Vic groaned as he settled into the rental truck's worn seat. He had to stop thinking like that. Where had his confidence gone?

His last girlfriend's face came to mind. They'd dated while he was in the military, and she'd stolen his heart and $12,000 of his hard-earned money. And what was worse, he'd overheard her talking on the phone to a friend and calling him Scarface.

Since then, being self-assured around any female felt as daunting as climbing Mount Everest.

Maybe he'd eventually find a trustworthy woman, and then dating again would be worthwhile.

Until then, he'd stay busy with work and far away from relationship trouble.

Rain and Lightning followed the trail from the lake into the silent green depths of the surrounding forest. For now, they were staying in her RV at one of the state park's campgrounds.

Pine needles covered the trail leading through a mixture of hardwood and pine trees. A cardinal flitted among the branches, its red feathers a stark contrast to the green.

At a dove's soft coo, Rain smiled. Her mom always said the dove was a sign of peace. Since coming to the area, Rain felt more at ease than she had in years.

The sellers had agreed to her offer for the house and property. Thanks to the inheritance money from her grandparents, the closing was fast-tracked, and in only five days, she would be an official homeowner.

Lightning spotted a squirrel, yanking the leash so hard that Rain almost lost her balance.

"Slow down, enjoy the day," she yelled.

As if disappointed, Lightning exhaled a weary puff of air and slowed his pace.

Rain chuckled and followed behind her sweet dog. She'd shared the real estate links with her parents and brother, and they were thrilled for her future.

Sonny had even driven down to view the property and was relieved Rain would finally settle in one place instead of traipsing all over the country.

Walking sticks in hand, an older couple's power-walk was punctuated by their labored breathing and the cheerful sound of "hello" as they passed.

Lightning glanced over his shoulder at Rain as though telling her they needed to pick up the pace.

"Okay, we can go faster." Rain kept at a light jog as he increased his speed.

She inhaled deeply, savoring the sharp scent of pine needles and the earthy aroma of the forest.

Her dog screeched to a stop, ears perked, his eyes fixated on something ahead.

The hair on the back of Rain's neck prickled as though alerting her to danger. Strange. She didn't see anything.

With a low growl, Lightning moved protectively close to her, his body tense.

Rain patted her dog's head. She knew there could be snakes, coyotes, and maybe even bears in South Carolina. She sure didn't want to be near whatever "it" was.

"Come on," she whispered.

As if protecting her, Lightning backed away, keeping

his body between her and whatever unseen thing had caught his attention.

Rain tried to act as though everything was fine, yet her feet had other ideas. She sprinted until she burst from the trees into the bright sunshine, and didn't stop running until she reached her RV and was safely inside.

Weird.

She hadn't felt that way in a long time.

Not since she was thirteen.

Her family had gone on a camping trip to the Smoky Mountains. She and Sonny had been laughing and talking, being goofy as they wandered down a trail. Sonny had frozen, gesturing for her to stay put with a raised hand. Back then, she had the same tingling sensation, the feeling of being watched. When they ran back to their parents, her father was wide-eyed and shaking. Even Mother had been upset.

Later that night, Rain overheard her parents' hushed voices—something about the danger and risks of their jobs.

The following week, their family moved to another town.

Chapter 6

Rain groaned as the rhythmic tap of Lightning's paws filled the RV, signaling he needed to get outside.

"Okay, give me a minute." Rain sat up in bed and ran her fingers through her hair, trying to smooth the unruly morning mess. She desperately needed a haircut. Hopefully, she could find a beauty shop in Crawdad Beach before her house closing.

Since her bedclothes were shorts and a top, all she had to do to get ready was slide her feet into her sneakers. Rain grabbed the leash and clipped it onto Lightning.

With a yawn, she pushed open the door and stepped into the early morning light. Stopping, she scanned the area. The sun had barely peeked over the horizon, and the campground was still nice and quiet.

Waking at the crack of dawn wasn't easy, but the calmness of the world outside made it worthwhile. She'd walk her dog and then get a shower before other campers started their day.

Lightning tugged on the leash as he led Rain to the designated dog area.

Last night she'd spent more time awake than asleep,

hoping she was doing the right thing buying a house, and puzzled by what had frightened her and her dog the afternoon before.

Why had she run when Lightning signaled something was ahead on the trail instead of finding out what, or who, it was?

Her parents had taught her and her brother martial arts. What she'd learned proved useful several times when faced with a date's unwelcome advances. She could take care of herself.

Lightning finished his business, Rain appropriately cleaned the area, then led him to a grassy area where he could run and play.

She unhooked his leash and let him go. Lightning yipped a happy bark, his tail wagging wildly as he ran circles around her.

While in college, she had confronted most of her problems head-on, until television and social media blasted her embarrassment to the world. Ever since she graduated from college, she'd been a restless vagabond, wandering from place to place.

However, no matter where she went, the memories of her past mistakes followed.

Perhaps if she stopped long enough, she could finally face her many failures and put an end to them chasing her.

Rain pictured herself striking a martial arts stance, as if ready to battle the ghostly remnants of the past.

Her shoulders slumped.

No matter how she fought, the past couldn't be changed.

Lightning flung himself in the grass and rolled onto his back, kicking his legs in the air. Her dog knew how to enjoy life. He didn't worry about what had happened yesterday or what might happen tomorrow.

Rain's foolish, cringe-worthy moments of her college years remained etched in time, no matter how much she wished they would disappear.

Today was a new day, and she needed to decide how she would live it.

She lay in the grass beside her dog and gazed up at the endless blue sky. For the past few years, she'd begged God for forgiveness for her sinful actions and that He would erase her many blunders from social media.

She believed God had forgiven her for her failures and embarrassing idiocy. And thankfully, those old social media posts had sunk so far down in the endless stream of content that they were practically gone from view.

It was time for her to close the door on yesterday and find joy in the present and future days. Forget work and her long to-do list; she needed to embrace the moment.

With a burst of energy, Rain jumped to her feet.

Lightning bounded up and danced around her.

She leaned closer to his furry face. "Let's go play!"

Rain took off running with her dog racing beside her.

She ran full throttle down the pine-needle-covered path, Lightning keeping stride with her.

Rain's cheeks hurt from smiling so wide as she and her dog bobbed and weaved among the trees.

Back behind her childhood home, she and the neighbor kids ran and played tag through the woods. Why had she forgotten to play?

A squirrel dropped from the branch in front of them. Rain screeched to a stop as a startled yip escaped Lightning.

With a twitch of the squirrel's furry tail, he sprang up the side of a tree, stopped on a branch overhead, and chattered his displeasure.

Her dog's gaze swung to Rain as if he couldn't believe the rudeness of the varmint.

She chuckled and motioned for Lightning to follow her back to the RV. Before her house closing, she needed to complete work projects and order items for her new home.

As the trees parted, they stepped out into the sunshine. Rain slowed as she watched a young couple and their two children by the lake.

The dad, with a gentle smile, worked patiently with his little boy, guiding his small hands as the dad taught him to fish. The mom, talking sweetly to her daughter, sat on a beach towel, braiding her little girl's hair.

A longing washed over Rain as she turned back to her

RV. Her best friend had jokingly called Rain's parents the odd couple, not because they were mismatched, but because they were odd.

Her parents were sweet people, just different. Scientists with high IQs they often struggled to relate to the real world, including their own children.

They'd forget to gas up the cars, pick up groceries, and even forgot a few times to pick up Rain and her brother from school. Her parents would often forget to mow the grass, much to the chagrin of their neighbors, who took pride in their neatly trimmed lawns and landscaping.

Rain unlocked her RV, paused for Lightning to enter, then secured the door.

At least her childhood wasn't boring. Her father's workshop laboratory, located behind the house, was where he spent his evenings conducting experiments. Which sometimes resulted in some very strange-looking concoctions, and a few minor fires.

When her mother wasn't working, she read fiction, immersing herself in the stories and adopting the personalities and mannerisms of the characters she encountered on the pages. Her science-fiction phase was Rain's favorite. How many kids got to pretend their family lived on another planet?

Rain settled into the chair at her work desk. She was a misfit raised by misfits.

Had God, in His infinite wisdom, placed her in her interesting family and created her uniquely, just as He planned?

Perhaps it was time to embrace her quirky upbringing and stop trying to conform to society's notion of normalcy. Most of her embarrassing college choices stemmed from a lack of confidence or an attempt to conform to others' expectations.

She so wanted to overcome her insecurities and remember that her past mistakes didn't have to define her. She wanted to be who God created her to be and walk in her true identity in Christ as a child of a loving God.

Rain opened the Bible app on her computer and scrolled through verses she had bookmarked in the past that told of God's forgiveness, healing, restoration, new life, new opportunities, and His unfailing love.

Like a gentle rain, the words resonated within her, echoing in the depths of her soul, bringing hope and healing.

Rain wiped the happy tears from her eyes and grinned at Lightning. "My name is Rain E Day. I am a child of God, and I am proud to be a misfit."

As though agreeing with her statement, Lightning wagged his tail and let out a joyful bark.

Chapter 7

With the last two boxes in tow, Vic stepped into his loft apartment. He kicked the door closed behind him, then placed his belongings on the granite countertop in the kitchen.

That a small town had anything this nice still surprised him. His apartment had wood-beam ceilings, a stone fireplace, brick walls, and French doors that overlooked Main Street. He'd signed a six-month lease for the two-bedroom apartment, which was a significant upgrade from his last place and way more affordable.

Vic's family didn't understand his move. Last night, lying in his hotel room, he had wondered the same thing.

His mother had called, her tone laced with worry as she asked, "How will you ever meet a nice girl in a little town?" His dad had said Vic needed to be in a bigger city to find enough work, and his brother had accused Vic of running away.

Maybe he was.

His job kept him on the road, but returning to his hometown had been a problem. It wasn't his family he avoided, just the reminders of his stupidity.

Vic rubbed his hand across the scar on his face—the proof of his idiocy in assembling fireworks to surprise and impress his high school girlfriend.

The only thing that surprised anyone was when the fireworks ignited prematurely, flinging fragments into his face and the nearby area. The shrapnel left him with permanent facial scars and destroyed his girlfriend's parents' garage.

As a result, she ended their relationship. Her friends, along with many of their neighbors, gave him the cold shoulder. Instead of attending university after high school, as he and his girlfriend had planned, Vic joined the military.

He slumped onto his couch. When anyone got brave enough to ask about his scar, he didn't have a decent story, nothing about heroic acts or being injured in battle while serving his country. It was his own stupid fault.

Life had led him down a road he hadn't planned to travel. His parents said God had readjusted his pathway, and then would quote the verse about God working all things for the good.

At least during his time in the military, he'd earned a college degree and developed abilities that helped him make a nice living as a civilian. So, that had turned out okay.

Hopefully, his move to Crawdad Beach was a step in the right direction, and he wouldn't ever have to live in his hometown again.

Rain had called ahead and made an appointment at Curl and Dye Beauty Shop. With her house closing scheduled soon, she wanted to look nice.

After the embarrassment she experienced in college, Rain had dyed her hair blonde, cut it extremely short, and completed her university courses online. Thankfully, as her hair grew, it transitioned from short curls to long waves, and she allowed it to revert to its original dark brown color.

Now, her hair needed professional help to get back in shape.

Rain stepped into the salon, and the scent of hairspray and the gentle hum of conversation filled the air. A smiling blonde woman about her mom's age stepped toward her. "Welcome to Curl and Dye, can I help you?"

"Yes, I have an appointment with Hannah."

"Wonderful. You must be Rain. By the way, I love your name. I'm Wanda King. Follow me." Wanda led Rain to where a young woman about her age with dark, cascading hair and captivating green eyes waited at a stylist's chair. "Hannah Joy. I mean, Hannah Doss, this is Rain."

With a hairdryer buzzing in the background, they

exchanged greetings while Rain took a seat.

"You wanted a trim?" Hannah asked as her fingers moved through Rain's hair.

"Yeah, it's been a while since I had a professional haircut."

"Your hair is nice and thick. We'll start with a wash and then get your hair fixed up." Hannah led Rain to the sinks in the back, wrapped a towel around her shoulders, and snapped on a cape. "Are you here visiting?"

Rain gazed up at the stylist as she leaned her head back against the porcelain sink. "I'm staying at the campground for now and am closing on a house in the area in a few days."

"That's great. You'll love it here." With a soothing touch, Hannah wet Rain's hair and used shampoo to create a rich lather. "What brought you to Crawdad Beach?"

"Stella, a lady who helped me get rid of a website hacker, mentioned it was a great place to live. Do you know her?"

"I'm not sure. But I haven't been here very long." Hannah stopped for a moment and addressed one of the beauticians. "Daphne, do you know Stella?"

The spiky-red-haired woman turned toward them. "Of course. She's married to Wilder. He's the man who helped you, the one who looks like an older version of the actor, Sean Connery."

"That's right. Thanks." Hannah's fingers went back to washing Rain's hair. "I haven't met Stella, but I know her husband."

"A Sean Connery look-alike?" Rain grinned. "Now, I'm even more curious to meet Stella." She'd have to call her online friend and see if they could get together.

By the time Hannah finished, Rain could barely stand, much less walk, after the amazing wash and massage she'd received. She wobbled and settled into the chair. "That was the best wash I've ever had."

Hannah grinned. "I like to incorporate massage techniques."

"My hair follicles and scalp would yell 'bravo' if they weren't so relaxed."

"Thanks, I'll take that as a compliment." Hannah ran her fingers through Rain's hair. "You have beautiful curls when your hair's wet, but the thickness turns them into waves when dry, right?"

"Yeah. When I was younger, I kept it short, which meant it was a curly, untamed mess. I haven't done anything in a long time, so I think my split ends have split ends."

"Hannah," a white-haired gentleman came hurrying toward them. "Can I please find out what happened last night? Sorry to interrupt," the man said, his eyes flitting between Hannah and Rain.

"No worries," Rain said. "I'm in no hurry."

"You sure you don't mind?" Hannah asked.

"Not at all." Rain said.

Hannah pointed at the man. "This is Chester Taylor. Chester, this is Rain. She's moving to our area."

"Nice to meet you, and welcome to Crawdad Beach," the man smiled as he nodded her way, then turned his attention back to Hannah. "Henry couldn't be here this morning, but he's curious too."

The receptionist and the other stylists all came running over, saying they wanted to hear the story. Even the other customers leaned closer.

Hannah combed Rain's hair while she talked. "Well, the meeting with Johan's son, Augustine, went well. He's nice." She turned her gaze to Rain. "I met my half-brother for the first time last night."

Rain wasn't sure how to respond to that statement. If she had a half-brother she hadn't met, it would have been because her parents had forgotten they had another kid.

Hannah gazed back at Chester and the other ladies. "So, anyway. He wants to stay in touch, and even apologized for his dad and what he'd done. I told him it wasn't his fault. Then he said his mom wants to meet me."

Chester's eyes widened with a gasp. "You're kidding. That's surprising."

The other women in the shop all nodded in astonishment.

"I'm surprised, too," Hannah continued, "but

Augustine said his mom always wanted a daughter. And she knows that what Francesca did wasn't my fault. That I'm not to blame for what happened."

Rain wanted to ask questions about what was going on, but just sat there listening.

Hannah picked up the scissors and started trimming the back of Rain's hair. "Augustine and his mom are both Christians and said they've forgiven what happened and wanted to move forward. It's probably helpful that Johan is out of the picture."

Chester made a whistling sound. "That's incredible. I'm happy for you. So are you going to meet the woman?"

"Thanks. I'm not sure. Maybe? I don't know."

"Are they going to share the family fortune with you?" the spiky-red-haired beautician asked.

Hannah puffed out a laugh. "I highly doubt that's going to happen."

"Well, whatever happens next, we'll be praying for you," Wanda said.

The others nodded in agreement.

Tears welled in Hannah's eyes. "Thank you all. I'm so glad God brought me here."

"We're glad, too." Wanda embraced Hannah. "We'll let you get back to work."

Hannah took a moment to compose herself before continuing to trim Rain's hair. "I'm sorry about the interruption." Hannah's green eyes gave an apologetic look.

"I don't mind," Rain said. She appreciated hearing what Hannah shared about her half-brother and his mother's forgiveness for whatever had happened, as well as their desire to move forward. She needed to do the same. Forgive herself, forgive others, and move forward.

Through the mirror in front of her, Rain gazed at Hannah. "Sounds like you've had an interesting life."

"Yeah, it's been a wild ride. But, I had a great childhood," Hannah smiled as she pointed to a photo of a smiling black family with one white girl, Hannah, happily standing in the middle of them. "Mama D gave me such a loving home."

"Nice. My parents were loving too, just quirkly different."

One of Hannah's eyebrows rose. "Quirkly?"

"Yep," Rain nodded, "my parents are kind of like the old movie The Absent-minded Professor on steroids."

"So, I'm guessing your childhood could have been on a sitcom," Hannah remarked with a smile. "Since you're moving to town, I'd love to get together."

"I'd like that. Thanks." Rain grinned.

"Great, I'll get you my number before you leave."

Rain smiled as the conversation continued. It looked like she'd found a friend before she even closed on her house.

Chapter 8

It was official: Rain had computer-office envy.

Yesterday afternoon, after getting her haircut, she spent a few hours at Stella's house. Her online friend, who was now her in-person friend, was a semi-retired cyber spy whose husband bore a striking resemblance to the older version of Sean Connery.

Stella's home office, equipped with a wall of computer screens and computers, was a tech-lover's paradise.

Rain sighed as she sat at the small desk in her small RV, working on her way-too-small computer. As soon as she got into her house, she was investing in new equipment for her business. She smiled, imagining her office with upgraded computers and big monitors that would make her work much easier.

Aside from enjoying meeting Hannah and then spending time with Stella, Crawdad Beach's interesting characteristics made Rain believe it was the perfect place to live. The residents embraced a cartoon crawdad as their mascot, and most of the businesses' names were humorous and quirky.

To top off the oddity, Rain had seen an older woman wearing a velveteen purple jogging suit riding a pin-striped riding lawnmower down Main Street at a snail's pace. Except from the look on the woman's face, she believed she was street racing. Plus, Rain had seen a young couple walking a humongous cat that looked like a cross between a mountain lion and a Persian.

Yep, the friendly town looked like the perfect place for her to settle.

Rain completed the job for a customer, emailed the invoice, and then turned to Lightning. "Want to go for a walk?"

With an exuberant bark, her dog sprang to his feet and sprinted to the door.

As he danced in place, Rain clipped on his leash, then grabbed her backpack. "Let's go explore."

The trail she chose started at a pavilion and meandered through a wooded area; the thick forest cover and the gentle terrain made for a leisurely stroll.

Lightning paused, his ears perked. Rain stopped and followed his line of sight. In the distance, two fawns stood frozen, their big brown eyes fixed on her and her dog.

Their tails flipped up, and the deer vanished into the depths of the forest.

Rain patted her dog's head. "Good boy for not going after them."

Lightning huffed out air as if annoyed he couldn't give

chase.

She led him away from the deer. The alternative path didn't have trail markings, so Rain stopped, trying to find her direction. The distant caw of a crow broke the silence, followed by the cheerful tweet of a bird close to where they stood.

Rain grinned, remembering a cartoon she watched as a kid that had a dawn chorus of birds and animals greeting the day. It wasn't the crack of dawn, but it was lovely to hear the quiet symphony of birds and the gentle breeze moving through the leaves.

A small chime of a text message came from her phone in her backpack. Rain took it out and checked. Her mom had sent something.

Weird.

The text was a string of numbers.

Another chime came with a message from her brother asking if Rain had received a strange text from their mom. Instead of going back and forth, she called him.

While they talked, trying to figure out if it was a joke or something else, Lightning's ears perked, and a low growl rumbled from deep within his chest as he moved closer to where Rain stood.

She scanned the path ahead and the surrounding trees. The strange feeling of being watched caused the hair on her arms to stand on end in response. Rain didn't see anyone, but an unsettling buzzing sound came from above.

Lightning didn't even look up. Still growling, he kept his attention focused on the trail in front of them.

"Hey, I gotta go," Rain whispered into her cell. "I'm on a trail at the state park, and Lightning's acting weird. I'll call you when I get back to the RV."

Vic skillfully guided his drone through the sky, meticulously surveying the property. During his filming, he always kept an eye out for anything that might add interest for his client and their potential buyers.

Yesterday afternoon, he stopped by a real estate office and offered his services. The realtor, Fushia Gates, was excited to take her business to the next level. They'd signed a contract assigning Vic twelve tasks involving aerial photography and videography of homes and properties to place on the realtor website.

Vic had given her a lower price for his work so that he could establish a foothold in the area. Hopefully, Mrs. Gates would recommend his services to others.

He'd already surveyed and filmed four smaller properties. This would be his biggest one.

Following a review of his notes, Vic sent the drone upwards, steering it above the road that rimmed the north and east sides. A barbed-wire fence next to the state park marked the remaining thirty-five acres.

Vic zoomed in to film around a barn and a small pond. Something moving in the grass caught his eye, and he lowered the drone to investigate. A small eastern cottontail froze long enough for him to get a cute shot of the little grayish-brown bunny.

He had invested more money to ensure his drone operated as quietly as possible, especially for moments like these, since his first drone had sounded like a flying lawnmower.

He directed his machine back above the trees to follow the barbed-wire fence and spotted something moving in the trees outside of the property.

A man wearing a camouflage vest with a state-of-the-art camera appeared to be observing a subject. Was he a nature photographer?

Vic maneuvered his drone, its long-range camera lens capturing the scene to gain a clearer perspective. Curious about what the man might be photographing, Vic checked the surrounding area for wildlife.

Instead, he spotted a woman and her dog.

As he stared at his screen, he leaned closer to get a better look. That was the same woman he'd saved from the falls.

Vic moved the drone back to monitor the dark-haired man. An uneasy feeling crawled over Vic as the guy stayed behind trees, maneuvering to get closer to the woman and her dog.

The man, whoever he was, was silently observing her from the shadows. As he readjusted his camera, Vic spotted a holstered pistol inside the man's vest.

Not good. The man might have more plans than just photographing the woman.

Vic growled and steeled his resolve. His drone might be destroyed, but there was no way he would let that woman be hurt.

He readied his equipment to distract the man and, if necessary, to attack.

Chapter 9

With a whir, a large black drone emerged from the sky, hovered in front of Rain for a nanosecond, then zipped down the trail following the direction her growling dog faced.

What on earth?

With a sudden pull, Lightning tugged on the leash, dragging her backwards toward the campsite.

Gunshots echoed, sharp and sudden, through the silent air.

Rain turned and ran, the unknown causing a chilling sensation down her spine. Her feet pounded the ground as they raced and weaved through the forest.

Trees closed around her. Branches grabbed at her legs, her arms, her head.

A bird screeched and darted in front of her.

She stifled a scream, her hand clamped over her mouth.

Her elbow knocked against a tree, spinning her sideways. Rain stumbled, regained her footing, the pressure on the leash pulling her forward.

They burst into the sunshine.

Rain sprinted until they reached the van, her lungs burning as she unlocked the RV door.

Hurrying inside, her heart still pounding, she locked up.

Thank goodness her blinds were still closed.

Leaning over, she focused on calming the frantic rhythm of her heart. Lightning looked worried as he leaned against her legs. She patted his furry head, then peered out the blinds of her side window. The campers and RVs around her were still the same ones. Nothing seemed out of the ordinary.

Who was shooting? And could someone be shooting at her?

People had hated her for causing the loss of the college football game, but it had been years since anyone was angry enough to want to harm her. Wasn't it?

Rain shook off that thought. Where did that drone come from? Lightning hadn't seemed upset at the flying robot, only at whatever was further down the trail. Had the drone dropped out of the sky to protect her?

If that was the case, she'd been saved from plummeting over the falls, as well as a potential shooter. Maybe this time her guardian angel had been disguised as a drone. Although she preferred a handsome scar-faced angel, she'd take whatever God gave her.

Wanting to share her latest disturbing adventure, she dialed her brother and told him about the drone and the shots fired.

"Call the police!" he yelled and hung up.

Maybe she should be more worried. Rain dialed 911 and explained the situation.

After the call, she phoned her brother again. "The police are on their way."

"Good," Sonny said. "Sit tight and stay locked inside. I figured out the numbers Mom sent. They're coordinates for a partially ruined castle in Switzerland."

"Do you think Mom and Dad are sightseeing?"

"Not sure. Neither of them answers their phones. I called where they work, and Mom and Dad haven't been in for a few days."

Rain tapped her chin. It wasn't strange for her parents not to contact them, but missing work was a different matter. They'd often forget about their kids but never their jobs. "What if Mom had been reading a novel and got trapped in a weird story, dragging Dad in one of her goofy adventures?"

"A possibility, but not likely." Sonny paused. "I've had some weird vibes, feeling like I was being watched."

The disturbing factor skyrocketed.

Her parents might be missing, and both she and her brother were being watched. Rain sank into a chair and raked her hand through her hair. "This doesn't make sense. Why would anyone want to hurt our parents or us?"

Sonny was silent for a moment. "Mom and Dad are

involved in top-secret medical research."

Rain's chest tightened. "What? Like spy stuff?"

"Something along those lines. I've known for a while." Sonny's quiet voice was barely audible.

Rain knew her parents were extremely intelligent, but she never thought they were involved in anything top-secret. That was like a movie, not her weird, quirky life. "Why didn't they tell me?"

"They didn't want you to worry."

"Well, I'm worried now!" Rain vaulted to her feet and paced back and forth in her small space. "What do we do? Should I fly to Switzerland to find them?"

"Sit tight. Do *not* go anywhere. Dad gave me a phone number in case anything happened to them or one of us. I'll see what I find out and let you know." He disconnected the call.

Rain rubbed her forehead. What was going on? Her world was tilting with the new information. How long had her parents been involved in that kind of medical research?

Maybe that's why they had her and her brother take martial arts. Maybe that's why they moved when she was a teenager. Maybe that's why they were always telling her to be careful. A zillion maybes zinged through her mind.

Good grief. She'd been raised by spies.

Rain peered again out the window. A police cruiser stopped, and a tall, blonde-haired officer got out and approached her RV.

What was she going to tell him?

Well, she could tell about Lightning getting upset, feeling someone was watching her, and hearing the shots.

What about the drone?

If it had protected her, who would have done that? And why was it there?

Maybe her forgetful parents were fine; the drone was just someone having fun, and the gunshots came from a wayward hunter, with no sinister intent.

At least she hoped so, because if not...

A chill slithered down her spine as she considered the alternative. Her entire family might be in danger.

Vic kneeled, picked up his wounded drone from the forest floor, and ran his fingers over the shattered propellers. At least his camera was still intact.

The man, woman, and dog were all long gone. Which made sense, since it had taken a while for him to arrive at the location where his drone dropped.

Could that man have been stalking the woman? What was his justification for being armed and shooting the drone?

Everything the man had done appeared suspicious.

Vic got back in his Jeep and drove to Crawdad Beach.

He'd drop by the police station and tell them what he'd witnessed. His video had captured the man's movements, including his watching the woman and then shooting the drone.

Hopefully, the police would identify the man and discover what he was doing.

A few minutes later, Vic parked, carried his drone and camera, and opened the police station door.

Stepping inside, the woman he'd seen in the forest turned toward him.

Staring at his drone, her eyes widened, and she pointed at Vic. "That's him!"

Chapter 10

With the woman's finger aimed directly at him, Vic froze in the police station doorway.

A silver-haired officer's intense gaze and a tall blonde officer's unwavering stare fixed on Vic.

He gripped his drone tight and hoped the video would show he'd done nothing wrong.

The attractive woman stood still for a moment, then she approached him. "It's you." Her tone was filled with wonder, as if he were someone special. Her blue eyes searched his. "You are the one who saved me that day at the falls."

With heat rising up his back, Vic dipped his head in acknowledgment. "Yes."

"And you used your drone to keep me safe." She said it as a statement, not a question.

At his nod, she smiled. "Thank you." She placed her hand on his cheek, and it settled right on top of his scar. "You're my handsome hero angel."

Vic swallowed hard, his eyes stinging as he fought back his embarrassment. No one had touched his scar and called him handsome. And definitely no one ever called him an angel or a hero.

"I'm Rain Day," the woman said.

At her interesting name, he tried to stop his grin, but couldn't.

One of her eyebrows quirked as she returned his smile. "Don't worry. I know it's a funny name."

Mortified that she'd touched him, Rain snatched her hand from the man's cheek. She wasn't in the habit of being affectionate, especially with strangers, but how often would she have an opportunity to touch her guardian angel?

"I'm Vic. Vic Caine." His gaze lingered on her face, as if trying to memorize her features.

"Nice to officially meet you, Vic Caine. Thank you for saving me at the falls and again today."

"You're welcome," he mumbled as his gaze dropped to the floor.

How could someone so handsome seem embarrassed by her comments? Then again, she had laid her hand on his cheek, right on top of his very cool scar.

"Son, can we ask you a few questions?" The silver-haired police chief asked.

Vic's gaze turned from Rain's to where the officer stood waiting. "Yes, my camera recorded what happened."

"Chief Weaver here," the older man said, then pointed to the other policeman. "And this is Officer Gabriel."

Rain followed Vic to where Chief Weaver stood waiting. He motioned for them to sit in the chairs in front of his desk. With a sidelong glance at her hero, Rain settled into her seat as he sat beside her.

The officer fixed his gaze on Vic, scrutinizing him. "Can you explain what you were doing with that drone?"

"I'm a property surveyor. I was photographing and videotaping for the realtor, Fushia Gates. My drone is damaged, but the camera is still intact. I have a recording showing what happened."

"I know Mrs. Gates, and I'm aware of the property." The officer's serious gaze moved to his drone. "I need you to download what you recorded."

Vic unhooked his camera, removed the memory card, and handed it to Officer Gabriel. "I noticed the man slinking around, and then when I saw Rain and her dog, I was worried the guy was up to no good."

Chief's eyes shifted to Rain, and his eyes softened before he returned his gaze to Vic. "I see."

Gabriel plugged the memory card into a laptop and then set it on the desk. Vic brought up the video, and in a few moments, showed the property, even pausing on a cute bunny, before the drone zoomed up to follow the camouflaged man.

Rain's skin prickled as the man watched her from behind a tree. The drone moved to show her and Lightning walking straight toward Camo Man until her dog stopped.

The drone zoomed down, and the man pulled a pistol from his vest and fired at the drone. As it plummeted, the camera kept filming, while the man rushed off and vanished into the woods.

Whoever that man was, he had been watching her, and he was armed. Rubbing the goose pimples rising on her arms, Rain glanced at Vic. "Thank you."

He ducked his head in acknowledgment. "You're welcome."

"Ms. Day," Chief Weaver said. "Do you have any idea who the man is?"

Vic rewound the video to stop where the guy's face was clearly visible.

She stared at the screen. The guy had dark hair and dark eyes, but nothing seemed familiar. Rain shook her head. "I don't think I've ever seen him before."

The chief's gaze gentled. "Do you have any idea why he might have been watching you?"

Besides being a creep, maybe it had something to do with her parents. Should she say anything about them or their jobs?

"Ms. Day, anything you can share would be helpful." Chief Weaver said.

"I can step aside," Vic said as he rose to his feet. "If you want to talk in private."

Since Vic had rescued her twice, surely he would be safe. Then again, what if he was near her both times because he was part of a group that had abducted her parents and was watching her and Sonny?

Officer Gabriel motioned with his chin. "Vic, why don't you come with me and make an official statement?"

"Sure." Vic gave Rain a gentle smile, then followed the officer to another room.

Rain leaned towards the chief. "I don't know who that man is, the one in the forest, but I found out my parents might be missing." She lowered her voice. "They are involved in some top-secret medical research."

The officer made a note, then his gaze flicked to where Vic sat with the other policeman, and then returned to her. "What do you know about the drone operator?"

"A few weeks ago, I slipped and fell into a river and was almost swept over the falls. Vic saved me. I didn't know it was him until today, but I recognized his eyes and his scar. Then, he saved me again today."

"Interesting." The chief wrote something in a notebook, then his eyes locked with hers. "So, Mr. Caine just happened to be in both places?"

"Yeah, I guess so." She looked over at Vic.

Was his presence in both locations simply a coincidence or something more ominous?

Chapter 11

As uncomfortable as it was to be sitting in a police station, based on the glares coming from Chief Weaver and Rain, Vic's halo had fallen off and smashed on the floor.

At least he'd been a handsome hero angel for a few minutes.

Officer Gabriel excused himself and walked over to Chief Weaver. From their whispered conversation and the not-so-friendly glances toward Vic, they assumed he'd done something wrong.

Strange that he'd been where Rain needed help on two occasions in two locations. Maybe the police were thinking his presence wasn't only a coincidence.

To help prove his innocence, Vic opened the email app on his phone and scrolled to find the information and invoice from when he'd surveyed the property near the river and falls.

As soon as Gabriel returned, Vic handed over his phone. "This is proof I was where Rain fell into the river because of work and nothing else. And I'm sure Mrs. Gates will be happy to confirm she hired me to film that property."

The officer scrolled through the email and attached invoice. "Looks legit, but we'll check." He jotted information on a notepad. "Where are you staying?"

"I'm in the loft apartments. 2B." Vic kept his mouth shut before he finished saying something smart-aleck like 2B or not 2B, that is the question.

"What brought you to Crawdad Beach?" Gabriel asked.

"I wanted to move to a smaller town. My friend, Marcus, suggested I'd like it here."

Gabriel's eyes met his. "Marcus Paterson?"

"Yeah. You know him?"

"Yes, can Marcus vouch for you?"

"Sure. We've been online friends for several years."

Gabriel made another note. "I'll need your previous address."

Vic provided that information, followed by details about his military service, role, and honorable discharge.

He waited as the officer continued to make notes. Vic bent towards the desk. "I know it seems strange that I was there both times Rain was in trouble, but it was just a fluke. Besides that, if I were doing something wrong, I wouldn't come to the police station to show you my video. Maybe being in both locations was a God-thing." He hadn't meant to voice that last thought aloud.

"Perhaps." Gabriel stared at him, his brow furrowed. "Give me a minute." He took Vic's phone and walked to another room.

Vic glanced to where Rain was still sitting. Had it been a God-thing that he was there the two times she needed help?

He wanted to believe God still had good plans for him. After all the mistakes he'd made, being called a hero felt good, even if it was only for a few minutes.

If God was watching over Rain, maybe God was also watching over him. Could it be true? As though he were just rubbing his eyes, Vic took a moment to pray for guidance and safety for him and Rain.

When he glanced up, Rain turned her attention his way, and a faint smile touched her lips.

Maybe there was hope.

Gabriel returned. "Marcus and Mrs. Gates vouched for you, and I did a quick check on your military service. Although I believe you're telling the truth, stay in the area."

"Planning on it. I have properties to film near town. Am I free to go?"

"Yes, we'll be in touch."

Vic stood. "Please let me know if I can help in any other way."

"You can take your equipment. We'll call if we have any more questions." The officer rose to his feet and gave him a firm handshake. "Thank you for your service."

"Thanks." Vic pulled back his shoulders as he walked

to the door.

He hadn't been heroically wounded in combat, but perhaps God had actually used him to make a positive difference in someone's life.

Rain watched as Vic gathered his equipment, while Officer Gabriel came over to talk to Chief Weaver.

She wanted to believe Vic was a good guy. Lightning hadn't been worried about him that day at the falls or about his drone. Dogs were pretty intelligent about that kind of thing, and Lightning seemed to have a sixth sense with people. If her dog trusted Vic and his drone, maybe she should, too.

"Ms. Day, I believe we have all we need from you for now," Chief Weaver said. "We'll continue searching for the man, and I've also sent a few inquiries about your parents."

"You can do that?"

The chief's eyes held a twinkle of amusement. "Crawdad Beach might be small, but it's home to incredible people, from ex-military personnel to security specialists with top-notch cyber skills."

"Like Stella?"

"You know her?"

"Yes," Rain said. "She helped fix a website issue. I met

her in person the other day."

"Do you have any objections to our contacting Stella for help with looking for your parents? She and her husband are very adept with security issues."

"That would be great. Thank you. The more, the better." Maybe everything would be okay, and they'd find out her parents had gone exploring and just forgotten their phones.

"We can also offer you protection, if you'd like."

Rain shook her head. "I'm sure I'll be fine." At least she hoped she wouldn't have any more incidents. She'd be more careful and aware of her surroundings, and she sure wouldn't be taking any more walks in the woods.

"If you have any other problems, just call." Chief Weaver rose to his feet and handed Rain a business card with the direct numbers of the station, Chief Weaver, and Gabriel.

"I will. Thank you." As she got to her feet, Rain slipped the card into the back pocket.

Vic, drone and camera in hand, stood waiting by the exit. "I hope you know I was trying to help."

"I figured that out. I think the officers also believe you. Thank you for all you've done for me."

"My pleasure." He held the door open for her, then walked next to her on the sidewalk. "Can I buy you a cup of coffee, something from the bakery, or lunch at Tiddlywinks?"

As she turned towards him, he averted his eyes. Why was Vic nervous and unsure around her? He was a great-looking guy, and from his actions, it was clear that he was very kind and thoughtful.

A distraction from her problems would be helpful. And since Lightning was lounging in the air-conditioned RV, he wouldn't miss her.

Rain waited until Vic looked up. "I'm hungry for lunch, so the restaurant would be nice."

A smile brightened his face. "Great. Let me drop off my equipment."

She waited until he placed his belongings in the back of a black Jeep Wrangler, then fell in step beside him.

It was time to find out about her mysterious hero, Vic Caine.

Chapter 12

Rain's stomach rumbled at the delicious smells as she scanned the Tiddlywinks restaurant menu. A crawdad wearing a chef's hat sat at the top of the list of their food offerings. Although the town was fond of crawfish, she noticed the item wasn't on the menu.

She glanced at Vic sitting across from her. "Have you eaten here before?"

He nodded. "I live only a few doors away; it's simpler to come here than cook something on my own. From what I hear, everything on the menu is good."

A waitress delivered glasses of ice water and stood by their table. Her friendly gaze moved between him and Rain. "What can I get y'all?"

After they placed their order, Rain gave Vic a curious glance. "What brought you to Crawdad Beach?"

"A friend said it was a great place to live." He didn't seem uncomfortable about her question, but didn't offer additional information. "How about you?"

"Same thing. Friend recommendation. Plus, I wanted to be close enough to my brother but not too close as to get in his hair. He's still in the newlywed phase. Way too much lovey-dovey stuff." She paused. "Not that I disapprove." Her cheeks heated at that statement.

To give herself time to cool down from making that embarrassing comment, Rain carefully removed the silverware from its napkin and took her time unrolling and placing the utensils in front of her, then put the napkin on her lap.

She looked up and noticed Vic looking at her, a playful glint in his eyes. "Can I ask you a personal question?"

Not sure what he might ask, Rain took a sip of ice water before answering. "Maybe."

"Fair enough. How did you come by your name?"

"My parents are sweet people, but they are a bit unique. I was born on a rainy day. My brother was born on a sunless day and therefore was named Sonny Les Day."

Vic grinned, and a slight indentation of a dimple formed on the cheek that wasn't marked by his scar. "Good thing you weren't born on a holiday. They could have named you Holly."

A man with a dimple and a sense of humor made him even more appealing. "True. I am grateful my name isn't even more unusual. However, my brother's wife's name is Holly."

Vic's cheeks flushed with unmistakable embarrassment. "Sorry about joking about that name."

Rain gave him a reassuring smile. "No apology necessary. We're used to the jokes."

Vic's expression turned more serious as he leaned toward her. "I know you talked to the police, but do you have any idea about that guy in the woods?"

"I don't have a clue. I don't think I've ever seen him before. So, why did you use your drone to go after him?"

"He seemed suspicious. I zoomed closer to stop your progress and then to let him know someone was watching him."

"Thank you for doing that. I'm sorry your drone got shot. Could I pay for a new one?"

"No." Vic held up a hand. "Don't worry. I can get it fixed, and I have a spare in my apartment. I'm just glad you're okay."

She grinned as she gazed at him. His eyes weren't blue like hers; they were a deeper blue, like the water in Oregon's Crater Lake. "You have a habit of showing up when I need you. Thank you." If only Vic and his drone had whisked her away from her embarrassing moment at the football game.

"I'm grateful I could help." The furrow in his brow creased. "I overheard you say something about your parents. Are they okay?"

Should she say anything? Rain wrapped her hands around her cool water glass. "They might be missing."

"How can I help?"

"Thank you for the kind offer. Chief Weaver is contacting people. Mom and Dad have been living in Switzerland for the last couple of years."

Vic tilted his head, searching her eyes. "With all that's going on, I don't understand how you're so calm. Most women I know would be a lot more emotional."

The waitress brought their meals, placing the plates on the table.

To give herself time to answer, Rain waited until the server left before meeting Vic's curious gaze. "I'm not the meltdown type. I hate drama."

She picked up her fork. "I'm hoping and praying that my parents are off on an adventure and just forgot their phones, and the guy in the woods isn't anything I need to be concerned about again."

Even as the words left her lips, she couldn't convince herself they were true.

While they ate, Vic wondered about the woman he'd rescued. Despite Rain's calm demeanor, the tiny quiver in her voice had been a giveaway. She was nervous.

Hoping to lighten the mood, Vic tried to think of something else. "What's your dog's name?"

Rain's tight shoulders eased. "Lightning."

"He seems like a friendly dog."

She puffed out a scoff. "I wouldn't say that. Lightning has left his mark on several people. He can sense things. Since he didn't attack you that day at the falls, that tells me he thought you were an okay guy."

"I'm grateful I passed his test." Vic felt, sensed, someone watching before he turned his attention to the left of their table. The biggest, tallest, muscular man he'd ever seen towered over them.

The man's eyes locked on Vic for a brief moment, then turned to Rain. "Chief Weaver and Stella sent me. My name is Valentino Bandino. Rain Day, I am here to help."

Vic detected a subtle Italian accent infusing the man's speech.

Pausing her fork midair, Rain's eyes went wide as she stared up at the man. "Thank you," her voice squeaked.

"May I join you?" Before a single response, Valentino pulled out the chair and sat. He leaned toward her but kept a respectable distance. "We've made inquiries about your parents and the man in the woods. A co-worker of mine is in Switzerland and is traveling to the coordinates you received."

Rain's gaze flitted to Vic before returning to Valentino. "How did you know about that?"

"There are many of us in town with connections. I also talked to your brother."

"You know Sonny?"

One of Valentino's shoulders rose and fell in a

nonchalant shrug. "The world is not as large as some might think."

Sensing Rain's discomfort, Vic pulled his shoulders back and hoped he looked tough. "Why are you getting involved?"

Valentino turned his head in his direction. "I'm known as the Eliminator." His lips twitched. "I eliminate problems."

Rain's eyebrows raised to her hairline as her gaze bounced back and forth between them. "How much do you charge?"

A flicker of warmth softened the big man's gaze. "No payment is required for a fellow Crawdadian."

She shifted in her seat. "I haven't moved here yet."

"Your house will close soon." Valentino rose to his feet. "I'll be in touch. I sent my contact information to your phone."

A chime came from Rain's cell as the massive man walked away. She checked the message and held up her phone toward Vic. "Looks like The Eliminator is on the case."

"I'm glad he's on our side," Vic mumbled. "Are you okay?"

Rain moved her food around her plate. "Yeah, sure. Just another regular day. I may have a stalker, or worse. Mom and Dad might be missing, and the biggest man on the planet is going to eliminate my problems."

Vic didn't know whether to chuckle or hold her hand to provide comfort. Instead, he picked up his fork. "I've heard of him, the Eliminator."

Rain glanced up. "You have?"

"Back in the military, there were rumors." Vic contemplated the information about the secretive man and his covert team, known for resolving problems in non-lethal ways.

"What kind of rumors?"

Vic quirked an eyebrow. "Let's just say your problems will be handled by professionals who operate within the boundaries of the law."

A look of relief spread across Rain's face. "Thank you for letting me know. I didn't figure Stella and the police would have sent Valentino if he were a criminal. Still, someone that big is..."

"Intimidating?"

"To put it mildly." She paused, her eyes lingering on him. "Thank you for being my hero."

Vic gave a quick nod. "I'm grateful I was there to help." Lord willing, he hoped she'd always think of him as a hero.

He sent up a silent prayer with only one word: *Please.*

Chapter 13

Rain sat at her RV desk, designing a book cover for one of her clients. With daily advances in technology and innovation, she could create almost anything using her graphics editor and artificial intelligence.

Content with the adorable characters she created for the author's western novel, Rain completed the draft and sent it to the client via email.

She sighed and leaned back in her chair. Lunch with Vic had gone great. They'd talked for several hours before he needed to get to his next assignment. After exchanging phone numbers, he promised to call soon.

She found herself irresistibly pulled towards Vic. Around him, she felt safe, seen, protected. His eyes held vulnerability and insecurity that resonated with her. Though she didn't ask about his scar, he occasionally angled his face away, as if trying to conceal the injury. She wanted to tell him he didn't need to hide his handsome face. She loved his look, and his very cool scar.

During their time together, Vic shared the details of why he was in both locations when she needed rescuing. They both agreed that it seemed more than a coincidence.

Had God orchestrated her rescues and meeting Vic? If so, why? Was it for her, him, or both of them?

Rain recalled two Bible verses: that every good thing comes from God, and God causes all things to work together for the good of those who love Him.

What interesting thoughts. It wasn't as though she spent time reading her Bible, which made her feel guilty, especially since her parents were missing.

Her mom used to tape verses on the bathroom mirror for her and Sonny to read. Rain sighed. Why had she forgotten that?

Lightning, holding the leash in his teeth, nudged her with his nose.

Rain got him ready, put her cell in her back pocket, and peeked out the RV windows. Besides getting darker, everything looked okay, and no one seemed to be lurking about the campground.

The humid air of late evening clung to her as she stepped outside. Menacing clouds hung above the western horizon, hinting at an approaching storm.

Two older gentlemen carrying fishing poles and their tackle boxes greeted her as they walked past.

A low rumble of thunder echoed in the distance. Rain hurried with Lightning to the dog walk area.

She'd check her weather app when she got back— experiencing storms while in an RV was not fun.

A misty blast of cool wind almost knocked her down.

Thank goodness she'd soon have a home on solid ground.

Her dog finished his business, and she cleaned the area. Even Lightning seemed in a hurry. They sprinted back to the RV, rain drumming on their heads and soaking their clothes.

Safely inside, she dried them both off. Opening her weather app, Rain checked the radar. Whew, this storm could be a doozy.

Should she find shelter? But leaving Lightning wasn't an option. He didn't like storms, and she didn't enjoy bad weather any more than he did.

A text message came from her brother.

Parents' location: Amstachtingen Castle, a privately held Swiss castle. One part occupied; the other in ruins. Valentino's team investigating.

Why would her parents be there?

Rain checked online for information. The castle, originally built in the 12th century in the Swiss mountains, had changed hands throughout the generations. It was now owned by a company called the Chimerastein Corporation.

Who were they?

She did a quick search of the corporation.

Medical research.

Interesting. Were her parents working for them, or had the company kidnapped her mom and dad?

Surely not.

Nothing made sense. Okay, some of it made sense, but exactly how did Valentino and Sonny know one another? Is that the contact Dad had given her brother?

A contact living in Crawdad Beach would be an oddity, to say the least. Of course, anyone called The Eliminator residing in a small town made no sense either.

She needed answers. Rain placed a call to her brother. No answer.

Strange.

Another text popped up. Her brother said he'd call soon.

Why didn't he just answer? Had something happened?

Deafening rain and a roar of thunder shook the RV. Lightning barked as though telling it to stop. A bright flash followed by a deep rumble caused him to whimper and scramble for safety beneath her desk.

The van shuddered as a gust of wind howled. Something slammed against the side of the RV, and hail pelted the roof.

With the storm raging outside, maybe she should take cover. Rain shut off her computer, then scooted next to her fur baby. As much as she hated hearing the storm, she hated even more that she was sitting on the floor with her dog instead of in Switzerland helping her parents.

Surely there was something she could do.

God had spared her life for a reason.

She wasn't there in person to help her parents, but

her prayers could reach anywhere. For the safety of herself and her family, Rain offered a prayer, and then another, and another.

Standing by the French doors in his apartment, Vic watched the storm's fury light the evening sky. He hoped Rain was staying safe. He couldn't imagine being in an RV in this kind of weather.

He liked Rain. The more they'd talked at the restaurant, the more comfortable he'd been. Besides her beauty, she was witty and intelligent. She didn't even seem bothered by his scar.

Tomorrow, he'd see if Rain would be interested in going out on a proper date. He felt hopeful, something he hadn't experienced in ages. He dared to imagine he might win her friendship, and perhaps eventually her heart.

Vic's lights flickered, then went out. He gazed at the main street through the sheets of rain.

Looked like everyone lost power. Good thing he'd shut down his computer.

He heard a distant sound, then it grew in intensity.

A siren.

Vic grabbed his cell and checked the weather app. A tornado warning had been issued.

He brought up the radar and zoomed in to take a

closer look. Every muscle in his body coiled tight.

Rain's campground lay directly in the tornado's path.

Chapter 14

"**Please,** God, let her be okay. Please."

Vic kept repeating the prayer over and over as he drove toward the campground. His frantic calls to Rain's number didn't even register a ring. The cell towers must be down.

In the light of his Jeep's headlights, leaves and branches covered the roadway in front of him. The closer he got to Rain's location, the more tornado destruction he saw.

Trees and power lines were down. Roofs ripped off houses and barns. In the darkness, he could make out the flashlights of people wandering around their property.

Vic's heart sank as he entered the state park. A group of trees stood like shredded toothpicks, their bare branches scraping the now clear night sky. He followed the road to the campground area. Mangled tents and pop-up campers blocked the way.

Vic parked, grabbed his flashlight, and got out. He didn't know which RV was Rain's, but she had said it was one of the smaller ones. Two bus-sized RVs were still standing, though battered by the wind-whipped debris.

At the sight of a small, overturned RV, Vic's stomach lurched. Splashing through puddles and rubble, he sprinted to the wreckage and searched for a way to get inside.

Though battered, the vehicle's windows were amazingly intact. With the RV lying on its side, the only door usable was on the driver's side, which now faced skyward.

With a grunt, Vic heaved himself up and tugged open the door. "Rain?"

He shone his flashlight, revealing belongings scattered around the vehicle. Using the edge of the topsy-turvy driver's seat as a handhold, he lowered himself into the mess. Papers, broken glasses and dishes, canned goods, pillows, blankets, along with a noxious smell coming from the tiny bathroom, made him cringe.

"Rain?"

What was her dog's name?

"Lightning?"

Vic continued searching, but there was no sign of her or the dog. Had she gone for shelter before the storm hit?

Vic stared up at the door above him. Getting in had been a breeze compared to the struggle of getting back out. He maneuvered into position and grabbed the armrest of the driver's seat.

The thing suddenly snapped, and he fell back.

His head slammed against something, and a flash of

pain shot through his skull.

Groaning, Vic pried open his eyes. He clutched the back of his head, where a throbbing pain centered, and felt the warm stickiness of blood.

Vic pushed himself up, gritting his teeth as he fought to stand. The beam of his flashlight was gone. He reached blindly, guided by feel, and tried again to disentangle himself from the overturned RV.

Bracing his feet, he strained, pulling himself upwards. Scrambling over the sideways driver's seat, he tumbled out the door and onto the roof.

He lay still and tried to catch his breath. Determined to find Rain, Vic rolled over, braced his hands, and dropped onto the soggy ground.

His stomach churned, keeping him from moving forward. He braced his hand against the RV to steady himself and waited until the nausea passed. He had to find Rain.

Vic sucked in a breath and pushed his legs to move. He weaved through the wreckage of the campsite. "Rain! Lightning!"

A pair of firm hands stopped his progress. "You need to come with me," a deep voice said.

Turning, Vic stared into the face of a tall, muscular fireman.

Vic waved him off. "You don't understand. I have to find Rain."

The firefighter gave a slight nod as he directed Vic to move in the other direction. "Right. It's okay now." The man's voice was calm and slow. "The storm is over. Let me get some help for your head."

"No, really, I'm fine. Help me find her. Rain and Lightning."

The fireman, with a firm grip, kept forcing Vic toward an ambulance. "You come with me, and I'll get you fixed up. The rain and lightning's gone, but it's okay." He whistled toward the paramedics, who were helping the injured. "Jake, I need your help with this one."

The men restrained Vic, preventing his escape, and sat him on the bed within the ambulance.

Vic tried to get to his feet, but they pressed him back down. "You don't understand; I'm not talking about the weather. I'm looking for Rain Day and her dog, Lightning."

The fireman and the paramedic exchanged glances.

"You got quite a head injury," the paramedic said in a low, soothing voice. "Do you know your name? Where you are?"

"Yes, I'm Vic Caine. We're in South Carolina. I'm fine. Let me go. I need to find Rain."

"Rain! Lightning!" He had to get away, find Rain, and make sure she wasn't hurt.

As the men conversed and organized their materials, Vic saw his chance. He vaulted to his feet.

Dizzy, his vision blurred around the edges.

All went black.

She'd heard Vic calling. Running with Lightning by her side, Rain arrived just as Vic collapsed onto the ambulance gurney.

In a panic, she pushed past a firefighter and a paramedic. "Vic." She gazed at the men. "Is he okay? What happened?"

"He's had a head injury. Kept yelling Rain and Lightning."

"I'm Rain Day, and that's my dog Lightning."

She could feel the men's gazes on her, filled with pity, as though she were mentally unwell. Thank goodness she had her backpack.

Rain grabbed her driver's license and shoved it at the fireman. "I really am Rain Day." She pointed at her dog. "And he's Lightning."

The man glanced at her license, then shot a grin in her direction. "Well, what do you know? I guess we owe your boyfriend an apology."

Rain tried not to roll her eyes at the men. Vic wasn't her boyfriend, but the thought was a nice one.

She placed her hand on top of his scar and prayed he would be okay.

Chapter 15

At the feel of a soft hand tracing the lines of his face, Vic forced open his eyes.

Rain was leaning over him, her damp hair falling in curls around her shoulders; her forehead etched with worry. "Hey, you."

He scanned her face for signs of injury. "You okay?"

"Yes, I'm fine." She gently caressed his forehead. "What happened to you?"

Vic grunted. "Minor incident while looking through your flipped-over RV."

Her forehead creased. "My RV's fine. It's parked next to a big motorhome that took the brunt of the storm."

At that embarrassing fact, Vic groaned.

"You were trying to rescue me again." Rain's voice whispered. She leaned down, and for a brief moment, her soft lips met his. "Thank you."

"You're welcome." Vic knew his grin was lopsided, but he didn't care.

A brief cough interrupted the moment. "Sorry to disturb the lovefest. Vic, if you think you can stand, I need to help other people."

"Yeah, sure." Still not feeling great, Vic stifled a groan as he sat up and got to his feet.

Rain's arm came around him, providing support. "I've got you."

Placing one arm around her shoulder, he leaned against her, not too much, just enough.

The paramedic and Rain helped Vic out of the ambulance.

Vic thanked the man and allowed Rain to lead him away.

Rain's worried glance swung toward him. "You need to stay with me until you're feeling well enough to drive."

Vic wouldn't argue. He could probably make it back to his apartment, but given the situation in the area and his condition, it was best to play it safe. Plus, he wouldn't mind spending time with Rain.

Her dog gently leaned against Vic's leg as though supporting his other side.

Rain grinned as she looked up at him. "I knew Lightning liked you. You're a good man, Vic Caine, and my favorite hero."

He cleared his throat, struggling against the emotion stuck there. What made Rain see him like that, and why didn't he believe her?

Rain helped Vic sit beside the little table inside her RV. That he'd searched inside another vehicle looking for her made her all warm and fuzzy inside. The man was so very sweet.

Thank goodness, her RV had a generator. Without asking if he wanted anything to drink, Rain handed Vic a bottle of water from her refrigerator, got one for herself, and then sat across from him. "Welcome to my home."

Vic's gaze quickly scanned the area, then returned to her face. "It's nice. And I am relieved the other place wasn't yours."

"Why?"

He grinned. "Let's just say there were several items that didn't fit someone as young as you."

Rain couldn't resist teasing him. "Would you be disappointed to know that I wear orthotics in my shoes, have a walking cane, and have been known to use lidocaine on my sore muscles?"

"Not in the least." His slow grin heated her cheeks.

She took a swig of her water. "So, Vic Caine, why are you so nice?"

A barely audible scoff escaped him. "I'm not that great," he mumbled.

"Hey, don't insult my hero friend."

"I'm no hero."

"Yes, you are. You've already saved me twice, and if I had been in trouble tonight, you would have saved me again." Rain tapped his muscular arm. "That is a hero. And I bet those aren't the only times you've done something heroic."

A grimace crossed his face as he gazed at the table. "Rain, I'm thankful God had me there those times to help you, but I've screwed up more times than I can count." He rubbed the scar on his face.

"We've all made mistakes. I bet yours wasn't broadcast on national television."

Vic turned his eyes back to her. "That would stink."

"Tell me about it." Rain took a deep breath. Might as well get it over with. She'd hate for her hero to discover the truth on his own.

Rain took her phone and scrolled to the link she kept to remind herself of her idiocy.

After she told him what had happened, she handed him the video.

He watched in silence before handing it back to her. "I've seen it before." His voice was gentle, not critical.

"Of course you have. The entire world probably has seen that video, maybe even a few alien planets."

Vic laid his hand on hers, the sensation sending a shiver down her spine. "You know what I thought when I first saw it? I wondered who the beautiful woman was and wished I had been there to help her back on her feet."

Throat burning at his kind comment, it took her a moment to respond. "I'm not surprised. That's who you are, Vic. You're a rescuer."

"Rain, I never had a hero moment until I met you." He pointed to his scar. "I got this by making a stupid mistake with fireworks, nothing heroic. My face got messed up, and my girlfriend's family garage burned to the ground."

She reached up and traced the raised edge of his scar with her fingertips. "Your face isn't messed up; you're a handsome man, and the scar is part of your story. I bet you were trying to do something nice for your girlfriend when it happened."

Vic gave a one-shoulder shrug. "Yeah, but it doesn't make a difference."

Rain sat back. "You're right; maybe it doesn't. The past is over. I don't know you very well, but I know you are a kind and thoughtful man who will always be my hero."

His eyes met hers, yet a shadow of doubt continued to cloud his expression.

"Vic, there are things I'm trying to learn. I want to believe in my true identity in Christ as a child of our loving God. I want to overcome my insecurities and remember that my past mistakes do not define me. You, too, are God's child. He loves you."

Rain softened her voice as she leaned closer to him. "And your past mistakes don't have to define you either."

Chapter 16

Vic lay in his bed staring at the dark ceiling. He believed God had given him the opportunity to help rescue Rain, but now he wondered if their multiple meetings had actually been more to rescue him.

The words she shared in her RV had washed over him like a healing rain. His past had troubled his mind and damaged his life for far too long.

God loved him, and God's mercies were new every morning; he needed to embrace those facts.

Vic traced the scar on his face. His high school plans had exploded in an instant, sending him in a different direction than he wanted. What if he looked at that situation from another perspective?

What if the accident had never happened, and he'd stayed with his girlfriend? She'd been a free spirit and a blast to be around, but their party days would've led him in the wrong direction. He'd heard she was still into the party scene.

Perhaps his scar should serve as a reminder not of his failures, but of God's saving him from a colossal mistake.

Morning light illuminated the scene of last night's storm. Broken branches, fallen leaves, shattered glass, and personal effects littered the campground.

Rain worked alongside park personnel, fellow campers, and a church group from Crawdad Beach. The church brought a van full of its members, armed with brooms, shovels, trash bags, and even a cooking trailer that provided hot meals and comfort.

She took a break and checked her cell. *Rats.* Still no signal. At least her RV's mobile satellite allowed her to stay in touch with Sonny. After Vic left last night, she'd emailed, letting her brother know she was okay. Unfortunately, he didn't have any updates about their parents.

"Hello, Rain Day."

She turned to face the smiling, white-haired gentleman she'd met at the beauty shop. "Hi, Mr. Taylor."

"Call me Chester." He motioned toward the woman with a bouffant hairdo standing next to him. "This is my wife, Maybelline."

"Nice to meet you." Maybelline's smile crinkled the corners of her eyes. "I've heard you're closing on a house soon."

With everything going on, Rain hadn't even thought about her property. "I hope so. I don't know whether it was damaged in the storm." What if it had been destroyed? She gave a nervous glance in that direction.

Chester followed her gaze. "Given the storm's route, your house should be safe." He motioned to the trail of devastation that led in the other direction.

Rain sent up a silent prayer that everything would be fine. Once she finished helping, she'd drive over and check.

The couple introduced Rain to their church friends, and they chatted as if she'd been part of the community for years.

"We'd love to have you visit our church." Maybelline's inviting smile was hard to resist.

Grinning, Chester moved closer. "Come early for free donuts and coffee in the lobby before the service."

"Thank you for the invitation. I just might do that." She did need to get back to church. She had a lot to be thankful for and a lot to pray about, especially regarding her parents.

The crunch of tires on the asphalt road drew Rain's attention. A police car slowly drove towards her and came to a stop.

Officer Gabriel stepped out. He grimaced as his eyes scanned the surroundings. He waved and greeted Chester and Maybelline, along with a few other people, before focusing on Rain. "Got a minute?"

With a mix of anticipation and worry, she hurried

toward him. "Is everything okay?"

Gabriel stood in a relaxed stance. "Downtown Crawdad Beach is fine. The storm caused property damage around the area, and a few people have injuries, but thankfully, no fatalities."

Since people were giving her curious looks, Rain leaned against the police car and tried to act casual. "That's good news, but you didn't just come here to tell me that; there's something more."

"It's about the man in camo." The officer lowered his voice. "He's been located and is in custody."

Her shoulders eased with relief as she looked up at him, her gaze meeting his. "That's good. Right?"

"Yes. The man was injured in the storm and found at a local hospital getting stitches on his arm. Chief Weaver has him in interrogation."

"Do you know why the man was watching me?"

"Not yet. We're continuing to look into that." A gentleness spread across Gabriel's face. "You don't have to worry. The man has outstanding arrest warrants with enough charges to send him away for a long time."

"That's good news, but I'd sure like to know why he was there."

"We should know soon. We'll keep you informed. Any news about your parents?"

A wave of moisture blurred Rain's vision. "Nothing yet."

Gabriel opened the driver's side door and gazed back at her. "We're praying for you and your folks."

"Thank you." At least Camo man was in custody, but why hadn't they found out his motive for watching her?

"Is everything okay?" Maybelline and Chester rushed toward her.

Rain rubbed her eyes like it was no big deal. "Yeah, sure."

"Gabriel's a good guy," Chester said. "But you let us know if there's anything we can do for you."

Maybelline placed her soft hand on Rain's arm. "We'll be praying for you."

Touched by everyone's kindness, Rain's bottom lip trembled. Her emotions were too close to the surface.

Trying to get herself together, she stooped to pick up a broken child's fishing rod. Her chest squeezed. Did that belong to the little boy she'd seen the other day? Had the storm hurt him and his family?

Rain searched the area, hoping to spot them. Relief flooded her when she saw them together, loading their belongings into a car.

Still, she wanted to cry.

Her parents were missing, she didn't know why the man had been watching her, and she was surrounded by the storm's devastation.

A sudden flash of black against the blue sky caught her attention.

A drone lowered in front of Rain and wiggled back and forth.

Vic. Her hero wasn't with her in person, yet he had pulled her back from the edge of becoming an emotional, blubbering mess.

She tried to muster up a smile as she waved to the attached camera. The drone dipped as though acknowledging her, then flew away.

Maybelline and Chester's eyes were both wide as they turned their gaze toward her.

"That belongs to Vic Caine. He moved into the loft apartments on Main Street. Have you met him yet?"

"No," Chester said, "but I heard a young man was helping Fushia Gates video her properties."

"That's Vic. He's such a nice guy."

As if sensing a hidden connection, Maybelline grinned. "We look forward to meeting him."

Rain got back to work, gathering debris. Was Vic using his drone to survey properties, or was he searching through the storm's destruction?

Either way, Rain had no doubt Vic was doing something good with his time.

She straightened her shoulders. She needed to pull herself together and focus on helping others. And she needed to remember to trust God, regardless of what happened.

Offering a silent prayer, Rain glanced skyward, yet

couldn't suppress an internal whimper.

Chapter 17

Up since dawn, Vic had spent his day helping people and surveying the damage for property owners and insurance adjusters. Although shocked by the carnage, he was relieved no one was seriously injured.

At a distraught little girl's request, Vic used his drone to scan the area surrounding her family's property. Crying, she'd run to Vic and begged him to help locate her missing little black and white dog.

He concentrated on keeping his drone low to the ground, his eyes watching for any movement.

When he'd flown over to check on Rain, she'd tried to smile, but she looked upset. Had she received news about the stalker or her parents?

Vic tried to stay focused on the search. Once he finished, he'd go check on Rain in person, make sure she was okay, and thank her for what she said last night.

A slight movement near a tree caught his attention. Shivering in a pile of leaves, Vic spotted the little dog.

Making a note of the location, he turned to where the family stood waiting. "I found him. He looks scared, but okay."

The little girl and her mother erupted in a sobbing meltdown. "Oh, thank you. Thank you."

The mom wiped her tears and peered over Vic's shoulder to see the screen. "That's him." She turned to the little girl. "He found Ruff."

Cheers erupted from the people who were removing fallen tree limbs from the family's yard.

The lady's husband stared over Vic's shoulder. "Can you zoom up so I can get an idea of where he is?"

Vic raised the drone, rotating the camera a full 360 degrees.

"I know where he is." The man dashed into the woods.

Keeping the drone over the little dog's location, Vic watched to make sure the man headed in the right direction.

After a short while, the family joyfully reunited with their soaked, tail-wagging pup, who was finally safe with his crying, rejoicing family.

Vic walked back to his Jeep. Seeing the family and their friends together made him long for a home, a wife, and a family of his own.

He placed his equipment in the back, then sat in his driver's seat. His fingers traced the scar on his face. Since the accident, he'd told himself no one would want a life with a scar-faced man. His high school girlfriend had made that clear, as well as the girl he'd dated while he was in the military.

Vic blew out a breath. His parents would often talk to him about the danger of negative self-talk, that his words mattered whether spoken internally or externally.

He knew that was true. The more he focused on his scar with negative thoughts and words, the more his self-confidence crumbled, the less hopeful he felt, and he imagined people viewed him unfavorably.

Vic started up his Jeep and drove to see Rain. He needed to remember that his injury was a testament to his deliverance from difficult relationships.

His identity was not a scar-faced man; he was a man loved by a loving God.

Arriving at Rain's campground, Vic parked near her vehicle. Only a few campers remained, and most of the storm's debris had been removed. A tow truck worked to put the tipped-over RV back on its wheels. The rhythmic growl of chainsaws reverberated through the nearby trees.

Vic tapped on Rain's door and waited. She didn't answer, and he couldn't hear any movement inside. As far as he knew, her vehicle was her sole means of getting around.

He took a step back and surveyed the area.

In the distance, he spotted Rain sitting in the grass near the lake. Her dog rested its head on his front paws, looking lazy and comfortable.

Rain's long, dark hair cascaded down her back as she stared at the water.

Enjoying the view of his beautiful friend, Vic took his time walking toward her.

Before Chester and Maybelline left, Rain told them the highlights of what was happening. The couple had encircled her in prayer.

With Rains' okay, Maybelline contacted the CBPT to join in praying for her and her family. Evidently, the Crawdad Beach Prayer Team consisted of devoted, godly, loving people who took prayer seriously and did not gossip.

Officer Gabriel had phoned to report that someone online had employed her stalker. Stella and a team of cybersecurity professionals were tracing who originated that request. And Valentino had let Rain know his contact was making progress in finding her parents.

Sitting in the soft grass, Rain pulled up her knees and encircled them with her arms. The lake's tiny ripples danced, mirroring the blue sky above.

God had protected her from a tornado and a stalker and provided her with people who were helping her and her family. She needed to trust God with all the rest.

Of course, trusting without worrying wasn't easy to

accomplish. And if she was still worrying, did that mean she wasn't trusting God?

Why couldn't life be easy and problem-free? Why did bad things happen? Why were her parents missing?

Rain thought about bopping her forehead to scatter her anxious thoughts to the wind. All the worrying and overthinking only caused her brain to spin and her head to hurt.

If she were Vic's drone, she'd fly above the problems and see what happened. Maybe that's what trusting God was like. Send the worries skyward to God in heaven and watch Him work.

Lightning sprang to his feet, his tail a blur of motion. Curious, Rain turned to see what had caught her dog's attention.

Vic waved in greeting as he approached. "Hey."

"Hey back at you." Rain patted the grass next to her. "I was just thinking about you." Well, at least she had been thinking about his drone.

"You were? I'm honored." Vic gave Lightning a big rubdown, and her dog's furry face looked like he was in pure bliss.

Vic settled next to Rain. "You doing okay?"

"Yeah, okayish."

"Still no word about your parents or that guy in the woods?"

Rain sighed. "No updates on my parents. The police

are still trying to figure out who hired Camo Man."

"It's hard not having answers." Vic turned his attention to the lake stretching out in front of them.

"Yeah, it stinks." Rain watched a motorboat in the distance fly across the water, the sound of its engine a low hum. Maybe she should have flown to Switzerland and searched for her parents herself.

"I want to thank you for what you said last night." Vic's kind words refocused Rain's thoughts.

She sifted through her foggy memory to remember what she'd said to him. Unsure of what it was exactly, she turned to look at him. "You're welcome for whatever it was."

"About remembering God's love is greater than our past mistakes. Thanks for helping me get clarity on a few things."

"If I said anything worthwhile, you can thank God."

He smiled. "I already did."

Rain stared into Vic's blue eyes, then her eyes trailed down to the curve of his lips.

What was she doing?

A wave of heat shot to her cheeks, and she quickly looked away.

Vic nudged her with his shoulder. His eyes sparkling, he stared at her lips for a moment, then gave her a questioning look. "Would you mind if I properly thanked you?"

At that excellent idea, Rain quirked an eyebrow. "I'm not one to pass up a good apology."

She sighed contentedly as Vic's lips brushed gently against hers. Whoa, baby, the man knew how to speak without saying a word. And she was totally enjoying what his lips were telling her.

No one had ever kissed her the way Vic kissed her. She tried to make sure her lips were speaking the same wonderful language as his. She really liked Vic, and from his sweet kisses, he liked her.

An irritating sound kept interrupting her thoughts. Was that her phone?

Rain groaned, reluctantly tearing herself away from Vic's wonderful kisses. A little lightheaded, she pulled the phone from her back pocket. She sucked in a breath. Sonny was calling.

Holding up one finger, she stood and motioned to Vic. "It's my brother. I need to get this."

Rain bit her bottom lip as Sonny told her the latest. They'd found her parents safe and unharmed, and several people were in custody for their kidnapping.

She broke down in tears, sobbing that it was finally over.

Vic vaulted to his feet, and his strong arms came around Rain, pulling her close.

All the pent-up fears and worries spilled out of her in a complete meltdown as she clung to her hero.

Vic gently tightened his grip around her.

With tears streaming down her face, she looked up at Vic, her breath coming in sharp intakes as she struggled to say something. "Mom and Dad are ... okay."

Chapter 18

The melody of birdsong serenaded the early morning light. Sipping her coffee, Rain sat in one of her camp chairs on the back porch of her new home while Lightning happily explored the backyard.

She slept like a baby, feeling safe and secure in her very own house. Or, as she liked to call it, her Baby Barndominium. Of course, after living in an RV, the place seemed enormous.

Since the previous homeowners had left the installed blinds and curtains, Rain had privacy to use the mattress from her RV to sleep on the floor of the master bedroom.

The last few days had been wild and amazing. She'd survived a tornado, her stalker and those who hired him were locked in jail, and her parents were safe and their captors in police custody.

And to top off the good news, she'd been blessed with Vic's sweet and wonderful kisses and the purchase of her first home.

Sonny and Holly had delivered Rain's stored items from their place, and it was great to see her brother and his wife, as well as to celebrate Mom and Dad's rescue.

Rain couldn't thank God enough for all her answered prayers.

A high trill from a bird sounded almost operatic. Rain grinned, imagining the feathered creature's wings stretched wide, chest puffed out, belting his morning song.

She'd read studies that birdsong helped plants awaken and grow. Listening to the tweets, warbles, operatic trills, and chirps, she wondered if maybe she should do the same.

If she sang and spoke to God, would her soul awaken and grow?

Despite her imperfect singing voice, her heart overflowed with gratitude to God.

Rain set down her coffee mug, opened the Bible app on her phone, and scrolled through verses about the morning.

She read aloud the verses. "In the morning, Lord, You will hear my voice; in the morning, I will present my prayer to You and be on the watch. Satisfy us in the morning with Your graciousness, that we may sing for joy and rejoice all our days. "

A dove's soft coo echoed from a nearby tree as if in agreement with the words.

Rain grinned and continued. "It is good to give thanks to the Lord and to sing praises to Your name, Most High; to declare Your goodness in the morning and Your faithfulness by night."

The rhythmic chirping of crickets joined in the chorus.

With a contented sigh, Rain read the next verse. "But as for me, I will sing of Your strength; yes, I will joyfully sing of Your faithfulness in the morning, for You have been my refuge and a place of refuge on the day of my distress."

She looked upward at the fluffy white clouds dotting the blue sky and whispered prayers of thanks for getting her safely through the storm.

Getting to her feet, Rain called Lightning. She had work that needed to be done, and then she needed to find furniture.

Four hours later, Rain arrived at Knick Knacks Antique Store. The little bell above the door chimed to announce her presence.

Her gaze swept over the abundance of furniture, glassware, antique jewelry, art, old toys, books, and various items that filled the old building.

"Good morning!" A young woman, probably not much older than Rain, with long brunette hair and big brown eyes, stood behind the counter. "Can I help you find anything?"

Rain smiled her way. "I just bought a house in the area and need furniture."

"Welcome to Crawdad Beach. I'm Grace Johnson. We have everything from repurposed, refinished, and even a few new creations." She came from behind the counter and walked toward her. "If you buy anything too big to carry yourself, we offer free delivery."

"Thank you, Grace. I'm Rain."

Grace gave her a quick smile. "Cool name. Come on, I'll show you what we have."

Rain followed Grace as they weaved their way around the store, examining various pieces of furniture.

"What brought you to our area?" Grace asked.

"I was looking for a place to settle, and Stella mentioned I might like it."

"Stella's great." Grace grinned. "I'm glad you took her advice. Did you buy a house in town?"

"I bought a small barndominium over by the State Park."

A flicker of worry showed in Grace's eyes. "Was your place okay with the storm?"

"Yeah, it was fine." Rain stopped at a refinished table and chairs that would look great in her kitchen dining area. The price tag was also perfect. "I was staying at the state park campground when the tornado hit."

"Oh my goodness, you okay?"

"Yes, thank God. And thankfully my RV didn't have any damage other than a few dents from flying debris."

Grace's eyes went wide. "You were in an RV when it hit?"

"Yes." Rain shuddered at the memory. "I will not do

that *ever* again."

"I'm grateful you're okay."

"Thanks, me too."

Grace continued chatting about the wonderful aspects of Crawdad Beach as Rain continued to look around the store.

Rain found two faux-leather chairs and a loveseat for the family room, a headboard made of pallet wood, along with a refinished dresser and nightstand for her bedroom. Until she ordered a new mattress online, she'd continue using her RV mattress.

She stopped to admire a live wood edge desk with steel legs that would be perfect for her new office.

"My husband's cousin, Tate, made that for us," Grace said. "Tate and his wife, Brooke, have several pieces here for sale and at his welding shop."

"I love it." Rain could fit several computer screens on top with plenty of room for her to work. "I'll take this and all the other furniture." She couldn't believe she'd found almost everything she needed at one stop.

Grace typed in a text. "My husband, Jeremy, is working at the shop today. I'll see when he and Tate can deliver your furniture." She motioned for her to follow to the counter. "You have made my day, Rain. Thank you."

She grinned. "That's my name. Rain Day."

"You're kidding?"

"Nope. And my brother is named Sonny."

Grace laughed, then her face flamed red. "I'm so sorry. I didn't mean to laugh."

"No worries. I'm used to it. You can imagine how interesting it was when my brother and I were kids playing in the neighborhood and Mom and Dad called us in for the night."

Grace bit her lip as if trying to hold back a chuckle. "Well, Rain Day, I'm glad you moved to Crawdad Beach."

"My sentiments exactly," Rain replied with a smile. Crawdad Beach kept getting better and better every day.

Vic emailed the invoice to his customer, then checked his online bank balance. Even with the expenses of his move, the month looked good.

Having lunch and dessert at Tiddlywinks would be a perfect way to celebrate. Better yet, he'd text Rain and see if she was up for joining him.

He typed the message on his cell.

Rain's quick 'yes' came with a happy face emoji, along with a comment that she was already in town and would meet him there.

Vic grabbed his keys and locked his apartment door behind him. Being with Rain was incredible. A vulnerability and tenderness in her expression had uncoiled the tightness in his chest, the carefully constructed walls he'd built around his heart crumbling with every breath in her presence.

He was falling for Rain, and this time, he didn't even care if his heart was broken again.

Well, he did.

Yet even with concerns about a possible heartache, Rain had already given him more confidence and a better outlook on life than he'd had in years.

Well, Rain and God had blessed him.

As he walked to the restaurant, Vic sent up a prayer that Rain would want more than just friendship.

Chapter 19

Rain's fingers intertwined with Vic's hand as they walked along the ocean shoreline—the sound of waves a gentle rhythm to their steps.

For the past three months, they'd shared most of their non-working hours together. With Vic, she'd laughed more than she had since she was a kid.

Lightning and Vic had bonded and greeted one another with a fist/paw bump before Vic would give her dog a rub down that would leave Lightning drooling in pleasure. Sonny and Holly liked Vic, and even her parents had video chatted with Rain when Vic was with her and had privately sent a message that they approved of him.

With a gentle breeze playing in her hair, Rain glanced over at her heroic boyfriend. His kindness and gentle nature were unlike anyone she had known before. The way he held and kissed her was incredible, sweet, and wonderful.

She was infatuated and head over heels in love with Vic Caine.

Warm air carried the sounds of laughter and conversation from those lounging on towels and beach chairs. Dodging waves, a group of children shrieked with joy and laughter. The thump of music pulsed, growing louder as they got closer to where teenagers were dancing.

Vic squeezed her fingers. "What you thinking?"

Rain grinned. "About a man named Vic Caine, and how much fun we have together."

"The feeling is mutual, Ms. Day." He wiggled his eyebrows and led her into the ocean waves.

Rain sucked in a breath as the water chilled her warm legs.

Vic gently directed her beyond the crashing waves. He stopped and pulled her into his arms, then gave her a soft, sweet, and slow kiss. "I love you, Rain Day."

Her heart happy dancing in her chest, she stared into his deep blue eyes. "I love you too, Vic Caine."

Rain rested her head on Vic's shoulder as they stood together in one another's arms, their bodies swaying in rhythm with the water's ebb and flow.

Vic hummed a tune that reverberated in his chest.

She raised her eyes to meet his. "Are you humming Amazing Grace?"

He smiled. "Absolutely. What God did to save me and bring you into my life is amazing."

"Aw, that's so sweet. I could say the same thing. I'm so grateful we're together." Rain rested her head back on his shoulder and hummed along with him.

Vic walked next to the woman he loved, her hand in his, as they retraced their steps to where he'd parked the Jeep.

Rain was stunning, delightful, kind, and loving, and as far as he could tell, perfect in every way. And she loved him.

Vic wanted to shout to everyone on the beach that Rain Day loved him.

Rain squeezed his fingers. "Best. Day. Ever."

He chuckled. "I agree."

A piercing cry came from a seagull in a noisy battle with another over a stolen piece of food.

A group of men who appeared to be part of a preppy fraternity approached. Their vulgar language and loud laughter a stark contrast to their polo shirts and designer shorts.

Vic gripped Rain's hand tighter as they walked past.

A blonde-haired guy, reeking of alcohol, stopped in front of Rain. His eyes narrowed. "It's you! You're the one who ruined the big game."

"Seriously?" Vic glared at him. "You're upset about something that happened years ago."

The guy jabbed his finger in front of Rain's face. "Because of you, I lost a $500.00 bet."

"Hey, back off." Vic shoved the guy back, positioning himself in front of Rain to keep her safe.

Vic barely dodged the guy's wild swing. He didn't want to get into a fistfight, not while Rain was watching.

The man's friends cheered and formed a circle around them.

Snarling like a wild animal, the blonde guy came at Vic again.

What did he have to do to get this guy to stop? Vic shoved the man, and he tumbled backward, landing with a thud on his backside.

With a growling grunt, the blonde-haired guy pushed off the sand and got back on his feet. "Won't fight me? You a chicken, scar-face?"

Vic, burning with anger, raced forward and, with full force, head-butted the jerk. The man fell to the ground, his eyes in a daze.

A fist slammed into Vic's cheek. He struggled to keep his balance, spinning to confront a black-haired guy with his fists raised.

Another man stepped toward Vic. "Come on, Scarface, let's see what you can do."

Before Vic could react, Rain kicked the guy in the face. Blood spurted from his nose as he collapsed in a heap on the sand.

Eyes wide with shock, Vic and the group of men all stared at Rain.

Rain huffed out a breath. "Vic, I know you could have smashed the rest of these drunk yahoos, but I will *not* stand here any longer and let anyone insult or assault my man."

Without another word, the men gathered their friends and left.

Vic chuckled. Well, what do you know? He was in love with a ninja woman.

He took Rain in his arms and kissed her. "You're my hero."

"And you're mine." Rain grinned, her blue eyes sparkling. "We make a good team, don't we?"

"The best."

Epilogue

Rain rolled over in bed, stretching and yawning before kissing her sweet husband. "Happy Anniversary."

Vic's eyes fluttered open, and a slow smile spread across his handsome face. "Happy first anniversary, Mrs. Caine."

She rested her head on his chest, listening to the steady rhythm of his heartbeat. Their engagement and the year they'd been married had zoomed past in a happy blur. "I still can't believe you dove into the water to save your drone."

He chuckled. "It carried your engagement ring. No way I was going to let that wash away."

Rain grinned as she admired her wedding band and diamond engagement ring sparkling in the early morning light. "I'm glad you were able to save the drone and the ring."

"I guess it wasn't my brightest idea to go back to where I first saw you to ask you to marry me."

"At least I didn't fall in the river this time. However, I am grateful I fell for you."

Vic kissed the top of her head. "I'm even more

grateful you said yes to marrying me."

With a joyous bark, Lightning bounced onto the bed, his furry face inches away, gazing at them both.

Rain giggled and sat up. "Looks like it's time for the Caine family to get moving." She held Vic's hand. "I have something else I want to tell you."

One of Vic's eyebrows raised as he sat up next to her. "And what might that be?"

She attempted to conceal the thrill bubbling inside her. "Candy, Sugar, or Walker will be coming to see us."

Vic gave her a curious look. "Who are they?"

Rain couldn't wait to see his reaction. "Candy Caine, Sugar Caine, or maybe even Walker Caine. Or whatever you want to name our first child."

With a whoop, Vic sprang to his feet, his eyes wide with excitement. "You're pregnant?"

"Yep. Three months today."

"A baby." Vic staggered back in a happy daze. "We're going to have a baby. I mean, you're going to have a baby. I'm going to be a father." He steadied himself against the headboard. "I'm going to be a daddy." His voice broke.

She wrapped her arms around her sweet husband. "You will be a wonderful daddy."

"And you will be a wonderful mom."

Rain nestled in Vic's embrace, closed her eyes and said a prayer of thanks for all God had done and the blessings that awaited them in the future.

Thank you for reading,

A Healing Rain

Lisa Buffaloe

Bible verses for the morning

"In the morning, Lord, You will hear my voice; in the morning, I will present my prayer to You and be on the watch," (Psalm 5:3).

"Satisfy us in the morning with Your graciousness, that we may sing for joy and rejoice all our days," (Psalm 90:14).

"It is good to give thanks to the Lord and to sing praises to Your name, Most High; to declare Your goodness in the morning and Your faithfulness by night," (Psalm 92:1-2).

"But as for me, I will sing of Your strength; yes, I will joyfully sing of Your faithfulness in the morning, for You have been my refuge and a place of refuge on the day of my distress," (Psalm 59:16).

Acknowledgments

I am deeply grateful to God for the immeasurable gift of salvation through His Son Jesus Christ. I'm also grateful for the countless times He rescues those in need, the healing and comfort He gives to the hurting, and the promise of eternal life in His loving family.

Dennis, thank you for being a loving, wonderful husband. Thank you for your prayers, support, and encouragement.

Patricia (Pacjac) Carroll, thank you again for your helpful feedback and for making the writing process loads of fun.

JoAnn Durgin, thank you for creating another beautiful cover. You are a sweet blessing to me and many others.

Jack Foster, thank you for sharing your creative Crawdad drawings used throughout the series. (Readers, please visit Jack at jackfosterart.com)

Thank you for taking the time to read *A Healing Rain.* If you enjoyed the novel, would you be so kind as to leave a positive review and share it with your friends?

Amazon https://amzn.to/4ltfEBA

Thank you!

About the Author

Lisa Buffaloe is a happily married mom, speaker, and multi-published author. She loves spending time with God, her sweet hubby, studying the Bible, writing, and enjoying nature.

Please visit Lisa at https://lisabuffaloe.com
Facebook https://facebook.com/lisabuffaloe
Twitter (X) https://x.com/lisabuffaloe
Instagram https://instagram.com/buffaloelisa
Amazon https://amzn.to/4ltfEBA

Books by Lisa
Fiction

Crawdad Beach Series
Each book may be enjoyed separately or as part of the series.

Visible, yet Hidden	*Mia Lets Go*
Running to Grace	*A New Paige*
Crystal's Journey Home	*Running from Shame*
A Baker's Heart	*Elise's New Song*
Stella's Heart Code	*A Found Joy*
River Steps Free	*A Healing Rain*

Hope and Grace Series
Each book may be enjoyed separately or as part of the series.

Nadia's Hope
Prodigal Nights
Writing Her Heart
The Discovery Chapter
Open Lens

Stand-alone novels

The Masterpiece Beneath
The Fortune
Grace for the Char-Baked

Non-Fiction

Float by Faith
Heart and Soul Medication
Time with The Timeless One
The Forgotten Resting Place
Present in His Presence
We Were Meant for Paradise
One Lit Step: Devotions for your journey
The Unnamed Devotional
Flying on His Wings
Unfailing Treasures
No Wound Too Deep For The Deep Love of Christ
Living Joyfully Free Devotional (Volumes 1 & 2)

A Healing Rain

Lisa Buffaloe

www.ingramcontent.com/pod-product-compliance
Lightning Source LLC
Chambersburg PA
CBHW070339130626
46556CB00007B/2931